R0061790598

03/2012

WHEN I OPENED MY EYES, I WAS SITTING IN A DUGOUT.

Perfect, I thought to myself. I had landed exactly where I wanted to be. It should be a simple matter to find Mickey Mantle, warn him about the silly drain, and get out of there.

But almost immediately, I sensed something had gone wrong.

This wasn't Yankee Stadium, it was obvious. I had seen "the House That Ruth Built" a million times on TV. It had those curved façades over the upper deck across the outfield. The ballpark I was in had no upper deck at all. The lower deck didn't even go all the way around. Somebody could hop right over the outfield fence from the street. No way was this a major-league ballpark.

I had been blown off course. Where was I?

Also by Dan Gutman

MICKEY
& Me

A Baseball Card Adventure

Dan Gutman

■ HarperTrophy®
An Imprint of HarperCollinsPublishers

Harper Trophy® is a registered trademark of
HarperCollins Publishers Inc.

Mickey & Me

Library of Congress Cataloging-in-Publication Data
Gutman, Dan.
    Mickey & me : a baseball card adventure / Dan Gutman.
        p.   cm.
    Summary: When Joe travels back in time to 1944, he meets the Milwaukee Chicks, one of the only
all-female professional baseball teams in the history of the game.
    ISBN 0-06-029247-4 — ISBN 0-06-029248-2 (lib. bdg.) — ISBN 0-06-447258-2 (pbk.)
    [1. Baseball—Fiction. 2. Baseball cards—Fiction. 3. Sex role—Fiction. 4. Time travel—Fiction.] I.
Title: Mickey and me. II. Title.
PZ7.G9846 Me 2003   2002005641
[Fic]—dc21   CIP
                                                                                             AC

First Harper Trophy edition, 2004
10 11 12 13   LP/CW   20 19 18 17 16 15 14
❖
Visit us on the World Wide Web!
www.harperchildrens.com

**Dedicated to Nina,
my all-American girl**

Acknowledgments

This book may have been possible without the help of Jim Nitz of the Milwaukee County Historical Society, but I don't know how. Thanks for everything, Jim! Also, a big thank-you to Dolly Brumfield White of the AAGPBL Player's Association; Joanne Pure of the Haddonfield Public Library; Rachel Kepner, Bill Francis, and Bill Burdick at the National Baseball Hall of Fame; Sue Macy; Rick Chapman; Jean Cobb; Tiby Eisen; Alma Ziegler; Vivian Anderson; Viola Thompson Griffin; Helen Steffes; Sarah Lonetto; Helen Hannah; John Ranz; and Dr. Scott Kolander.

Introduction

WITH A BASEBALL CARD IN MY HAND, I AM THE MOST powerful person in the world. With a card in my hand, I can do something the president of the United States can't do, the most intelligent genius on the planet can't do, the best athlete in the universe can't do.

I can travel through time.

Joe Stoshack

1

The Last Request

"YOUR FATHER HAS BEEN IN A CAR ACCIDENT."

I almost didn't hear the words. Or, if I heard them, I chose not to believe them.

"Did you hear me, Joey? I said your father has been in a car accident."

She used to call him "your dad." After they got divorced a few years ago, she switched to calling him "your father." My mom's voice came over the phone with a seriousness and urgency that I wasn't used to hearing.

Before the phone rang, I had been rushing to put on my Little League uniform. Running late, I was trying to jam my legs into my pants with my spikes on. I stopped.

"Is he okay?" I asked.

"He's alive," Mom replied. "That's all they told me."

"Was he drunk?" *Dad always liked his beer, sometimes a little too much,* I thought.

"I don't know."

"Was it his fault?"

"I don't know."

"Was he wearing a seat belt? You know the way he hates—"

"I don't know," my mother replied, cutting me off in mid-sentence. "Joey, listen to me carefully. I need to go pick up Aunt Liz and your cousin Samantha. I'll take them to the University of Louisville Hospital. You know where that is. I need you to ride your bike over there. I'll meet you at the emergency room waiting area. Have you got that?"

"I got it."

"Repeat it back to me."

"I got it, Mom."

"Take your baseball glove and stuff with you. You can go straight to your game."

"Okay."

"I'll be at the hospital as soon as I can."

When I hung up the phone, it was like I was in a trance. My game that afternoon—probably our most important game of the season—didn't matter much anymore. It's funny how something can seem so important, and then something else comes along that turns your whole world upside down and you feel silly for being worried about the first thing. Just a silly baseball game.

I never expected my dad to live forever, of

course. But he wasn't even forty years old! For the first time in my life, the thought seriously crossed my mind that he could die and I would have no father.

Mechanically, I finished putting on my Yellow Jackets uniform jersey, went downstairs, locked up the house, and hopped on my bike. The University of Louisville Hospital was two miles away. I didn't bother taking my bat or glove with me. There was no way I could play ball today.

The emergency room at the hospital had no bike rack. I dropped my bike on the grass by the front door and ran inside. My mother wasn't there yet. When I told the lady at the reception desk that my dad's name was Bill Stoshack, she directed me to Room 114 down the hall. It took a few minutes to find it.

"Your father is a very lucky man," I was told by a tall doctor in blue scrubs.

Dad didn't look very lucky to me. He was unconscious and had tubes running in and out of him, and all kinds of machines were beeping around the bed. His face was banged up and bandaged so I could barely recognize him.

"Is he gonna be okay?" I asked. I felt tears welling up in my eyes but fought them off.

"We hope so," the doctor said. "We won't know with certainty for a couple of days, after the swelling goes down."

My father was not drunk. But the driver of the

car that hit him was, according to the doctor. It had been a horrific head-on crash a few blocks from where my dad worked as a machine operator in downtown Louisville. Several other cars had been involved in the collision, and a bunch of people were hurt.

"We believe your father had a subdural hematoma," the doctor told me. "It's a blood clot between the skull and the brain. If he hadn't been wearing a seat belt, he would be dead for sure."

That was a shock to me. My dad always hated the seat belt law. He said it took away people's freedom.

An emergency operation had already been performed to drain fluid from inside my dad's skull, the doctor told me. There could be other problems. Dad was being given painkillers and drugs through an IV tube. A male nurse came into the room.

"He has been going in and out of consciousness," the doctor told us both as he made his way toward the door. "Don't be alarmed if he wakes up and says something that doesn't make sense. That's just the drugs talking. I need to check on some other patients, but I'll be back shortly."

I pulled up a chair next to the bed and leaned my head close to Dad's until I could hear him breathing softly.

"He'll be in good hands here," the nurse told me. I ignored him. What else was he going to say—*It looks like your father is going to die any minute*?

I took Dad's hand in mine. It was totally limp. He didn't squeeze my fingers at all, the way he usually did. But he opened his eyes.

"You okay, Dad?"

"Butch," he said quietly. He always called me Butch. "C'mere. . . . I need . . . to . . . tell . . . you . . . something."

I leaned closer.

"Mickey . . . Mantle," he whispered.

"Is your father a baseball fan?" the nurse asked.

"Yankee fan," I corrected him. "He loves the Yanks. What about Mickey Mantle, Dad?"

"His . . . card," Dad said. He was struggling to get each word out. "The . . . rookie . . . card."

I knew exactly what he meant. Mickey Mantle's 1951 rookie card was the most valuable card printed since World War II. It was worth more than $75,000. My dad had started me collecting baseball cards when I was little, and he taught me just about everything I knew about the hobby.

"Why is he telling you this?" asked the nurse.

"What about the Mantle rookie card, Dad?"

"I . . . have . . . one."

"You have one? Where did you get it?"

"Shhhh, listen," he said. "I . . . hid it. Under . . . the . . . floorboard. Left side . . . of . . . your . . . bed. Under . . . the . . . rug."

I realized immediately why he was telling me about the Mantle card. He thought he was going to die. My father never had much money. The Mantle card was going to be my inheritance.

"You're going to be fine, Dad," I assured him. "Fifty years from now you can give me that card."

"No," Dad croaked. "Write . . . this . . . down."

He looked very frail and weak, but he was summoning up the strength to speak. I grabbed a pen and pad from the drawer next to the bed.

"Go ahead, Dad."

"World Series. 1951. Game Two. Fifth inning. Willie Mays hit a soft fly ball to centerfield. DiMaggio caught it."

"So?" I asked, jotting down the information.

"Mantle was running over . . . to back up DiMaggio. . . . His right cleat got caught . . . on a drain cover. Mickey collapsed . . . like he'd been shot. They carried him off on a stretcher."

"Why did they have a drain in the middle of the outfield?" I asked. "That seems pretty stupid."

Dad shook his head, as if to say he had something more important to discuss.

"Before the accident, Mickey was the fastest player in the game. He could run to first base in three seconds. After, he was never the same. His legs were shot. Who knows how good he would have been if he hadn't stepped on that stupid drain? Who knows how many homers he would have hit, how many records he would have broken?"

I put the pen down. I had an idea of where Dad was heading.

"And you want me—"

**"Mickey collapsed like he'd been shot.
They carried him off on a stretcher."**

"To stop him," Dad said, completing the sentence. "I've been thinking about it for a long time, Butch. Go back to 1951. You can warn him. Should be easy. You know how. You're the only one who can do it. That's why I gave you the card."

Dad closed his eyes. He had used all his strength to say what he had to say.

"He's hallucinating," the nurse told me. "It sounds like he thinks you can travel through time."

"Ha-ha-ha." I laughed. "That's ridiculous."

In fact, I could travel through time . . . with baseball cards.

Ever since I was about five years old, I noticed that baseball cards had an effect on me that they didn't seem to have on other kids. When I picked up a card—particularly an old card—I felt a strange feeling in my fingertips. It was a tingling sensation, a gentle buzz that reminded me of the feeling you get when you brush a finger against a vibrating guitar string.

I discovered that if I held the card long enough, this tingling sensation would travel up my arm, across my body, and the next thing I knew, I would find myself in 1909, 1947, 1932, or whatever year was on the baseball card. The card, somehow, had transported me to another time and another place. I would always end up somewhere near the player on the front of the card.

This was my little secret. I had hardly told anybody about it.

My mom always says everybody has a "special gift." Some people are great musicians or brilliant mathematicians. Some people can fly planes or save people trapped in burning buildings. My special gift

9

was that I could use baseball cards to travel through time.

Dad opened his eyes.

"And get yourself a haircut," he murmured, closing his eyes again. "You look like a girl."

"He needs to rest," the nurse told me, escorting me to the door.

It seemed kind of silly, going back to 1951 to warn Mickey Mantle about some dumb drain cover hidden in the outfield of Yankee Stadium. But as I looked at my dad lying on the hospital bed, I had the feeling that this might be the last thing he would ever ask me to do. So I would try to fulfill his request.

Unfortunately, as it often happens in the imperfect science of time travel, things don't always turn out as you expect them to.

2

Benchwarmer

MY MOTHER AND MY AUNT WERE HURRYING DOWN THE hallway as I left my father's room. Mom kissed me on my forehead.

"How is he?" asked Aunt Liz, my father's older sister.

"He's sleeping," I reported. "But I talked with him. I think he's gonna be okay. He has a subdural hemasomething or other."

"Hematoma," said Mom, who is a nurse and knows stuff like that.

Aunt Liz hugged my mom, whose face was emotionless. I knew she had mixed feelings toward Dad. They had never really gotten along very well when they were married. But I always thought she still felt something for him. Otherwise, she wouldn't have come to the hospital at all.

To be perfectly honest about it, Dad and I didn't

always have the greatest relationship in the world either. He was an angry man, and he seemed to think he'd had more than his share of bad luck. Maybe he had. But in the last year or so—since I turned thirteen—we had begun feeling more comfortable around each other.

"We dropped your cousin Samantha off at the Little League field," Mom told me. "Can you bring her over to our house after your game and keep an eye on her tonight?"

"You mean I have to baby-sit?" I whined. "You said you were going to bring her to the hospital with you."

"We decided that Samantha is too young," Aunt Liz explained. "I don't think it would be a good idea for her to see Uncle Bill laid out in a hospital bed."

"Okay," I grumbled. I didn't particularly want to take care of my annoying nine-year-old cousin, but this was an emergency.

"I'll be home as soon as I can," Mom said. "But depending on your father's condition, we may stay with him in the hospital tonight. There are leftovers in the fridge for dinner. Don't pick up the phone or open the door. I don't care who it is. You're the man of the house. Be a good boy."

"I will, Mom."

"And get a hit, okay?" she said, messing up my hair with her fingers.

"I'll try."

I didn't tell my mother that I had decided not to play that day.

Louisville, Kentucky, is a big baseball town and has been for a long time. There was a major-league team here from 1876 until 1899. In fact, the National League was founded in Louisville, and the Louisville Slugger baseball bat was invented here. Today we have a big museum filled with bats used by the greatest players in baseball history.

But I wasn't thinking about bats, even as I rode my bike past the six-story-high baseball bat outside the Louisville Slugger Museum. I was thinking about my dad.

He could be dying right now, I thought. Maybe I should ride back to the hospital to be with him. It could be my last time to see him. Then again, he might be fine in a couple of days. And I had agreed to take my cousin home with me after the game.

When I skidded up to Dunn Field, our game was already in progress. In fact, I had missed three innings. According to the scoreboard, we were three runs behind Warehouse Video, the only team in the league that we never seemed to be able to beat. Because they had lost to a few of the weaker teams, we were ahead of them in the standings by one game. But if they beat us, Warehouse and the Yellow Jackets would be tied for first place.

"Where were you?"

Coach Tropiano came running over to me as soon as my kickstand touched the ground. He was a short man, only about five feet seven and not much taller than me. "We tried calling your house! We tried calling your mother at work!"

"My dad was in a car wreck," I explained. "We were at the hospital."

"Is he okay?" the coach asked, putting an arm on my shoulder. I think he had been going to yell at me for being late until he heard about my dad.

"I don't know," I replied. "I hope so."

"Will you be able to play, Joe?"

"I don't think I can, Coach."

I could tell he was disappointed, even though he was doing his best not to show it. One of the other coaches had gotten into trouble recently for yelling at a kid, so all the coaches were being extra careful to be sensitive and stuff.

The coach told me to take a seat on the bench. Our team was in the field, so the only kid on the bench was Robert Greene. He couldn't hit, throw, field, or run, but he did have one thing going for him—his mother was on the city council. Coach Tropiano usually put Robert in right field in late innings, where he could do the least damage. According to the league rules, every player has to play at least one inning or come to bat once in every game.

Robert was picking his nose and wiping the result on the inside brim of his cap. Our team had signs for stealing, bunting, and swinging away, but I didn't think that was one of them.

"Where's your glove, Stosh?" Robert asked me.

"Didn't bring it," I told him. "I'm not playing."

"You hurt?"

"Nah, my dad's in the hospital."

"That sucks," Robert said, and then resumed mining for nose gold.

I turned around to scan the bleachers. When I made eye contact with Cousin Samantha, she stuck out her tongue and wiggled her fingers in her ears at me.

The crack of a bat got my attention. One of the Warehouse Video players hit a long drive to left field. It sailed over Andrew Bakewell's head and bounced off the fence on one hop. The kid who hit the ball was fast, and he was tearing around the bases.

"Cutoff man!" I screamed, getting up off the bench. "Relay!"

Andrew chased down the ball and whipped it to Christian Dark, our shortstop and probably the best defensive player in the league.

By that time, the kid was rounding third and his coach was waving him home. Louie Borzone, our catcher, got into position for the play at the plate.

"Slide, Brendan!" somebody yelled from the bleachers.

Christian set himself and fired the ball home. Louie Borzone snared it on a hop just before the runner arrived. He braced himself for the collision and let the Brendan kid crash into him. Louie was the bigger of the two, and the Warehouse Video guy couldn't knock him over. Louie held the ball, and the ump called the kid out.

"All right!" Coach Tropiano yelled, slapping the guys on their backs as they ran off the field. "Way to hold 'em! Now let's get some runs!"

I felt something poking me through the fence behind our bench.

"How's Uncle Bill?"

It was my cousin Samantha. She was holding an ice-cream cone in one hand and a red loose-leaf notebook in the other. In the excitement, I had forgotten about my father in the hospital for a moment. Now that she had reminded me, I was sad all over again.

"He'll be okay, I think," I told her. "After the game I have to take you over to my house for the night."

"I don't need a baby-sitter," she said. "I can baby-sit for myself. And you know what?"

"What?"

"One time I had a baby-sitter and she made popcorn and she left the microwave on too long and you know what?"

"What?"

"It burned the popcorn and smoke was all over the place and it set off the smoke detector and you know what?"

"What?"

"The fire department came and you know what?"

"Listen, Samantha," I said, "can we talk about

this later? We're in the middle of a game here."

"I made a new bag of popcorn all by myself and gave some popcorn to the firefighters," she announced proudly. "So that's why I don't need a baby-sitter."

I told you she was annoying.

Samantha scampered back to the bleachers. Coach Tropiano looked over at me, but I wouldn't meet his eye. I was afraid he might ask me to pinch-hit.

The Yellow Jackets went down one, two, three in the fourth inning. Every time the coach looked over at me, I turned away or shook my head to let him know I didn't want to play.

"How come you're not playing, Stosh?" Alec Italiano asked.

"I don't feel too well," I replied, and it was the truth.

The score was still 6-3 when we got our last licks in the bottom of the sixth. With two outs, Alec and Andrew singled, and Louie walked to load the bases.

Coach Tropiano came over to me. This time he didn't just give me a look.

"Can you pinch-hit, Joe?" he asked. "An extra base hit will clear the bases and tie this game up."

The guys on the bench all turned to look at me.

"I'm sorry, Coach. . . . ," I said.

The coach mumbled something to himself and looked up and down the bench.

"Have you been in the game yet?" he asked Robert Greene.

"Nope."

"Grab yourself a bat and do something wonderful with it."

There were a few groans on the bench as Nose Picker Boy marched to the plate and proceeded to flail helplessly at three pitches that were so far over his head he couldn't have hit them if he'd been standing on a ladder.

That was the third out, and that was the ball game. The Warehouse Video players mobbed their pitcher as though he had just tossed a no-hitter. They were tied with us for first place now. After we shook hands with the other team, both coaches agreed to play again tomorrow afternoon to decide which team would be the Louisville Little League champions.

None of the guys said anything to me as they packed up their gear. But I knew what they were thinking. If I had come to the plate, I might have hit a double or triple to tie the game. I might have even homered to win it.

I was thinking the same thing. But with my mind on my dad and all, I just couldn't bring myself to play. I grabbed my bike and went to get my cousin and go home.

3

Boys and Girls

"HOW COME YOU DIDN'T PLAY, JOEY?" MY COUSIN Samantha asked as she gathered up her notebook. Then I began walking my bike home. She kicked a rock, her ponytail flipping back and forth, as she skipped beside me.

"I guess I just feel bad about my dad," I said. "I didn't think I'd be much good to the team."

"Too bad your parents are divorced," Samantha said. "My friend Jessie's parents got divorced and you know what?"

"What?"

"Her mom and dad hated each other so much, they used to throw stuff at each other."

"My folks were never like that," I said.

"Hey, Joey, you got a girlfriend?"

"What does that have to do with anything?"

"It doesn't," Samantha explained. "I changed the subject."

"No, I do not have a girlfriend." Not that I would have told her even if I did have a girlfriend.

"Ever been on a date with a girl?"

"No."

"Why not?" Samantha pressed. "My mom told me that boys and girls start getting interested in each other when they get to be twelve or thirteen and you're thirteen so you should be getting interested in girls right about now."

"Well I'm not," I lied.

"Do you like boys?"

"No!"

"Just asking! You said you're not interested in girls. If you're not interested in boys, what are you interested in?"

The truth was, there was this girl named Emily in one of my classes who I was very interested in. She was beautiful. But I wasn't going to tell Samantha I liked Emily. I hadn't even told Emily I liked Emily! I had never even spoken to Emily.

"I'm interested in baseball cards," I said, hoping that would be the end of the discussion.

"Do you have hair under your arms yet, Joey?"

"None of your business!"

She started tickling me and trying to peek at my armpits, but I grabbed her and tickled her back until she collapsed in a fit of giggles.

"It's all because of hormones, you know," she informed me. "When you reach puberty, hormones

20

go through your system and all these weird things start happening."

"Your mom told you all this?" I asked.

"No, I read it in a book I found hidden under some stuff in a drawer in her bedroom," she said. "And you know what?"

"What?"

"It even has pictures!"

"You're too young for that stuff," I said, making a mental note to check out my aunt's bedroom drawer the next time we went over for dinner.

I knew all about puberty. Our gym teacher had given all the boys in the class "the talk" at the end of fifth grade. You know the one I'm talking about. Each of us came home with a stick of deodorant.

"You know, I'm interested in baseball cards, too," Samantha told me.

"What does that have to do with hormones and puberty?"

"Nothing," she said. "I changed the subject again. And you know what?"

"What?"

"I've got my whole baseball card collection in this notebook. Wanna see it?"

"Maybe later."

We had just about reached my house. Samantha told me again how she didn't need any baby-sitter, going off on a long, involved story about the time her parents' car broke down so she was all alone for a night. I decided to make my special macaroni and cheese for the two of us.

"Girls used to play professional baseball, you know," Samantha said as I drained the noodles.

"Oh yeah?" I said. "Name one."

"Connie Wisniewski."

"Never heard of her."

"Never heard of her?" Samantha was outraged. "She was the best pitcher in the AAGPBL."

"The what?"

"The All-American Girls Professional Baseball League," Samantha said, as if any idiot would know that. "They played during World War Two when a lot of major-league players were away fighting. Didn't you ever see that movie *A League of Their Own*?"

"No," I replied, mixing the noodles with butter, milk, and the packet of cheese powder. Macaroni and cheese was my specialty. Well, to be honest, it was the only thing I had learned how to make.

Samantha dashed off to the living room and came back with the red notebook she had been carrying around with her.

"Is it later now?" she asked.

"Huh?"

"You said you would look at my baseball card collection later," she explained. "Is it later now?"

"I guess so," I replied as I scooped some mac and cheese into bowls for each of us.

She opened her notebook on the middle of the table, and I had to admit she wasn't making the whole thing up. Page after plastic page was filled with cards of female baseball players. The photos were all black-and-white—pictures of women with old-time hairstyles, wearing dresses, and holding bats and balls and gloves. They had funny names— Corky Clark, Peeps Pieper, Be Bop Vukovich. They were the strangest baseball cards I had ever seen, and I had seen them all.

"Look," Samantha pointed out. "Here's Connie Wisniewski. She's my favorite."

The page was labeled MILWAUKEE CHICKS, 1944. I turned the page to look at the back of the card. It said that Connie Wisniewski played nine seasons, winning 107 games while losing only 48. One year she went 33-9. Her nickname was "Iron Woman."

"If she was a guy," Samantha claimed, "Connie Wisniewski would be in the Baseball Hall of Fame today."

"If she was a guy," I snorted, "she couldn't make my Little League team today."

"That's a lie!"

"Oh, come on," I said. "Girls can't play baseball."

"Can too!"

I'd had some experience with this issue. When I was younger, there were usually a few girls on my Little League teams. By the time I reached what we call "the majors," most of them had switched to softball or dropped out entirely, and there were only two or three girls my age in the whole league. They couldn't hit for beans and they threw like, well . . . like girls. I think one of them was only on a team because she was the coach's daughter.

"My dad told me that men and women are fundamentally different," I explained to Samantha. "Men are bigger and stronger. We're naturally competitive. Girls don't like physical confrontations. You're afraid you'll get hurt. You need to be protected. That's why girls can't play baseball. It's all because of hormones and stuff."

"That's a lot of bull!" Samantha shouted. Then she reared back and punched me on my cheek.

"Owwww!" I yelled. She had taken me totally by surprise. I put my hands up just in case she might try to get another shot in.

"Well, my mother told me that the only reason

girls don't play baseball is because they aren't given the chance. Everybody is telling them that they're supposed to play softball."

I thought about arguing that point, but I was afraid she might sock me again, so I let it go. We had finished our macaroni and cheese, so I took the bowls to the sink.

"You know," Samantha said, "I can read with my eyes closed."

"Are you changing the subject again?" I asked.

"Watch." She slipped one of her baseball cards out of the plastic page and held it in front of her. Then she closed her eyes and began reading the statistics off the back of the card.

"You're peeking!" I laughed.

"No I'm not! I'm reading the words right through my eyelids!"

"That's pretty impressive," I said, humoring her. "You know what I can do with a baseball card?"

"What?"

"I can travel through time."

I'm not sure why I decided to tell her. It's not like I told everybody I met that I had this power. It wasn't any deep, dark secret or anything. I just figured anyone else would think I was crazy. But my cousin was kind of annoying, and I thought it would be cool to blow her mind.

"You cannot travel through time with a baseball card!"

"I can," I said. "The card works like a time

machine. It can take me back to the year on the card."

"Really?"

"Would you like a quick demonstration?"

"Sure!"

My baseball card collection was up in my room. I thought about which card I should use. I had been thinking about Roberto Clemente, Ty Cobb, Satchel Paige, Roger Maris. . . .

Then I remembered what my dad had said in the hospital. He'd hidden a Mickey Mantle rookie card in my room and asked me to warn Mickey about the drain cover at Yankee Stadium. I had almost forgotten about it.

"I have the perfect card," I told Samantha.

I ran up to my room, taking two steps at a time. An oval rug covered the floor near my bed. I slid it out of the way and poked around until I found a loose floorboard. It lifted easily. There was an envelope in the space below, with writing on the outside.

> Butch—you can use this more than I can.
> Give my regards to Mickey.
>
> Love,
> Dad

I ripped open the envelope and peeked inside. Sure enough, it was the famous Mantle rookie card, safely encased in a clear plastic holder. I had seen pictures of the card in magazines but never the real thing.

In my desk drawer were some unopened packs of new cards I had bought a few days before. I grabbed one pack and slipped it in my pocket. Just as an old card could take me back to the past, I needed a new card to return me to the present.

Clutching the Mickey Mantle card, I went down to the living room, where Samantha was leafing through her notebook on the couch.

"Is it like magic?" she asked, looking at the Mantle card.

"It's a lot like magic."

"How does it work? How long does it take? Does it hurt? What does it feel like? When will you come back?"

"Just watch," I instructed her. "I have to give a message to Mickey Mantle. I'll be back as soon as I can. If the phone or doorbell rings while I'm gone, ignore it."

I got comfortable on the couch and carefully slipped the Mantle card from its plastic holder. I closed my eyes.

"Is it working?" Samantha asked.

"Shhhhh . . ."

It took a few seconds, but soon I felt that familiar tingling sensation in my fingertips. It started out very gently and became stronger until my fingers felt like they were vibrating.

Then I felt a slight jolt, like a car switching gears. The feeling started to spread, first to my hands, and then up my arms to my shoulders. Then it washed down my chest like a wave crashing onto a beach, down my legs and to my toes. The whole time I was thinking about Mickey. There was a feeling of lightness, numbness. My body was undergoing a transformation. I couldn't have stopped it at that point if I had wanted to.

"Joey," Samantha said, "you look . . . lighter."

And then I felt myself disappear.

4

Slip Me a Mickey

WHEN I OPENED MY EYES, I WAS SITTING IN A DUGOUT.

Perfect, I thought to myself. I had landed exactly where I wanted to be. It should be a simple matter to find Mickey Mantle, warn him about the silly drain, and get out of there.

But almost immediately, I sensed something had gone wrong.

This wasn't Yankee Stadium, it was obvious. I had seen "the House That Ruth Built" a million times on TV. It had those curved façades over the upper deck across the outfield. The ballpark I was in had no upper deck at all. The lower deck didn't even go all the way around. Somebody could hop right over the outfield fence from the street. No way was this a major-league ballpark.

I had been blown off course. Where was I?

Looking around, I saw that the field wasn't what

I expected either. There was a regulation-sized baseball diamond, but the place was deserted.

Clearly, I had traveled through time. Everything was made of wood. The outfield scoreboard was one of those old-fashioned kinds in which somebody had to put up boards with numbers on them whenever a team scored a run. All the cars parked beyond the centerfield fence looked like PT Cruisers. There was even a horse tied up to a pole outside the left field stands.

This was all very weird.

There was a newspaper on the ground near my feet. The *Milwaukee Bulletin*. What was I doing in Milwaukee? I picked it up. The headline on the front page was about as large as I had ever seen.

EXTRA THE MILWAUKEE BULLETIN EXTRA

Sixty-second Year   Wednesday, June 7, 1944   4 Pages – Invasion Extra

Allies Begin Invasion; Attack Hits Normandy

The date on the paper was June 7, 1944, the day after D day. I guessed that it was yesterday's paper, which meant I had traveled to Milwaukee on June 8, 1944.

I knew a little bit about D day. The first R-rated movie my parents ever let me see was *Saving*

Private Ryan, which was all about D day. That was the day the Allies launched a huge invasion to take Europe back from Nazi Germany. It was one of the bloodiest battles of World War II.

I was seven years early and in the wrong town! Something must have gone wrong. Something always seemed to go wrong!

A small sign on the outfield fence said

BORCHERT FIELD
Home of the Milwaukee Brewers and Chicks

Brewers and Chicks?

The sun was sinking beyond the right field stands. The clock near the scoreboard said it was almost six o'clock, which was about the time I left, I estimated. I glanced around the dugout. There was a lineup card taped to the wall.

1. Petras, ss

2. Keagle, cf

3. Eisen, lf

4. Tetzlaff, 3b

5. Maguire, c

6. Klosowski, 1b

7. Whiting, rf

8. Ziegler, 2b

9. Wisniewski, p

None of the names sounded familiar to me until I got to that last one.

Wisniewski.

Where had I heard that name before? Then I remembered. Connie Wisniewski was the name of that lady pitcher my dopey cousin idolized! And that meant . . .

I looked at the baseball card in my hand.

She must have taken the Mickey Mantle card out of my fingers while I had my eyes closed and slipped one of her girly-girl baseball player cards in its place.

She tricked me, the little rat! She must have taken the Mickey Mantle card out of my fingers while I had my eyes closed and slipped one of her girly-girl baseball player cards in its place. That would account for that jolt I had felt while I was in the process of traveling back in time.

I turned the card over. This is what it said on the back:

Dorothy answered to "Mickey" because her style of play mirrored that of Hall of Famer Mickey Cochrane.

Oh, I'll kill her! When I get home, I'm going to destroy that little weasel! She slipped me a Mickey!

Okay, calm down, I kept telling myself. This is not so terrible. I've been in a lot worse situations. Like the time that crazy batboy tried to brain me with a bat when I went to meet Jackie Robinson in 1947. Or the time that gangster shot at me when I went to meet Shoeless Joe Jackson in 1919.

Samantha pulled a little prank on me, that's all. No harm done. It was pretty clever of her, actually, substituting a Mickey Maguire card for a Mickey Mantle card. I didn't know the little squirt had it in her.

There was a simple solution. I would just find a nice, quiet spot and travel back to my own time.

A door in the back of the dugout looked promising. The knob turned. I opened it and went inside to find an empty locker room. Perfect.

It was pretty dark in there, but I could read a handwritten sign on the wall.

All Games Canceled June 7
Because of D Day

I pulled my pack of new baseball cards out of my pocket and sat on the floor by an empty locker. Ripping open the pack, I knew I didn't have to be picky. Any card—superstar or benchwarmer—

would take me back to my own time.

I picked a card at random and closed my eyes. Soon the tingling sensation started to come.

That's when I heard a voice. Many voices, actually. Female voices. I opened my eyes.

And, brother, I want to tell you, I saw something that I will not forget for the rest of my life—a line of teenage girls coming out of a shower room, naked as the day they were born.

I dropped the baseball card. *Maybe I shouldn't be so hasty in getting back to my own time,* I decided. *I mean, what's the rush?*

There were tall ones, short ones, blondes, and brunettes. There must have been about ten or more. I didn't want to stop to count. How come you never have a camera with you when you need one?

Silently, I slipped the cards back in my pocket. I didn't breathe. A sneeze or cough at this moment would be disastrous. I refused to blink or I would miss a millisecond. I was drinking it all in, like I had stumbled upon an oasis in the desert.

When I was little, my parents took me to the Grand Canyon, and it was beautiful. Yosemite National Park was beautiful. People talk about the Eiffel Tower, the pyramids, the *Mona Lisa*. But I'm going to be honest with you. None of them could possibly compare with this.

Don't get me wrong. I had seen naked women before. Well, I had seen one naked woman before, twice. Her name was Katie Jackson, and she was

34

Shoeless Joe Jackson's wife. But that's another story, and it was only for about a half a second each time. This was different. This was my all-time fantasy. This had been my dream ever since I was, well, eleven.

This, I concluded, must be what heaven is like.

Then, of course, somebody had to go and flip on the lights.

"Eeeeeeeeeeeeeeeeeeeeeeeeeeeeeeeek! A man!"

5

Chicks and Chickens

"EEEEEEEEEEEEEEEEEEEEEEEEEEEEEEK!"

You would have thought a swarm of killer bees or a pack of man-eating bears had invaded the locker room. But it was just me, sitting on the floor and minding my own business. I put my hands over my ears to prevent my eardrums from exploding.

"There's a man in the locker room!" one of the girls shrieked.

Towels appeared out of nowhere. A magician could not have conjured up so many towels out of thin air so quickly. As I struggled to hold the after-image on my retinas of what I had seen, I cursed Thomas Edison for inventing the lightbulb and whoever it was who invented the towel.

The curtains were drawn. The show was over.

"It's just a boy," a very tall blond girl said. "Relax."

"Who are you?" a girl wearing glasses demanded as she wrapped a towel around herself. "What are you doing here? How long have you been hiding?"

"M-my name is Joe Stoshack," I stuttered, getting to my feet. I put my hands in the air so they would know I was harmless. "I was only hiding . . . I mean I've only been here for a few minutes. It was an accident. I just wanted a nice, quiet place where I could, uh, relax and—"

"I think he's cute," a very short blond girl said, stepping forward to pinch my cheek. I thought she was pretty cute too, and she was only about five foot two. "Let's keep him. Snookums, my name is Merle Keagle, but the fans call me the Blond Bombshell."

"Stop flirting with the boy, Merle," the tall blonde said.

"Everybody calls me Stosh," I said. My face must have been tomato red.

"Hi, Stosh!" Merle giggled.

They had gathered around me like I was a newborn panda at the zoo. One of the girls pushed her way through the crowd. She appeared to be a little older than the others, twenty-five or so. I felt as though I had seen her before somewhere, but I couldn't place her. She had dark eyes and brown hair, and she was a few inches taller than me.

"I'm Mickey Maguire," she said. "Are you the new mascot?"

I most certainly was not the new mascot. But I made the instant decision that being a mascot for this team might be a pretty good job to have.

"Yeah, I'm the new mascot," I lied.

"Terrific," Mickey said, pulling a box out of the locker next to hers. "Put this on."

I opened the box. Inside was a giant yellow chicken suit with a separate head.

"I have to wear this?"

"We're the Chicks." Mickey said the word slowly, like I might be dumb. "Our mascot is a chicken. What did you think you'd be wearing, an elephant costume?"

The girls got a good laugh over that. Mickey moved me over to her locker and turned me around so I couldn't see the girls putting on their uniforms. I slipped my legs into the chicken suit.

Somebody turned on a radio. The singer sounded like Frank Sinatra or one of those other old-time crooners my mom listens to from time to time just to annoy me.

"What happened to the last chicken?" I asked Mickey as I struggled to pull the zipper on the chicken suit past the feathers, which kept getting in the way.

"We ate him," Mickey cracked, letting out a laugh. "No, he quit actually. We scared him off."

Mickey's locker was filled with catcher's equipment, bandages, medicine, ice packs, and other medical supplies.

"Tape and guts keep me going," she said when she noticed me looking at her stuff.

There were two photographs taped up in her locker: one of a horse and the other of a guy wearing a military uniform.

"Is that your boyfriend?" I asked.

"My husband," she replied. "He's a corporal in the army. Overseas for two years now."

"Is he a part of the D day invasion?"

"No, thank goodness. Tom is stationed in Italy. At the end of every letter, he always writes, 'When the Allies take Rome, I'm coming home.'"

"Is that your horse?" I asked.

"Yup. That's Chico's Flame. I raised him myself. Got him hitched up beyond the left field fence. Do a good job and I'll give you a ride later."

I finally got the chicken costume on. The head attached to the body with a series of hooks. It was too tall for me to see out the eyes, but I could look and talk out of the mouth.

"You look like a real chicken," Mickey said, turning me around.

The girls were dressed in their uniforms now. I turned my chicken head until I found Merle, the girl who had said I was cute. To my eyes, she was the prettiest girl on the team. I thought I saw her flip me a wink.

Most of the girls were about my size—five foot five—with the exception of the really tall blonde. She was skinny, with long arms and legs. The girls were hanging around, doing crossword puzzles, putting on lipstick, and fixing their hair in the mirrors hanging from each locker.

Their uniform looked like it had been designed for dancing, not for playing baseball. It was a gray dress, with short sleeves, red trim, and a belt. On their feet were regular baseball spikes, and black socks that came up almost to the knees. Their caps had a red bill and a big *M* inside a yellow circle. On the front of the uniform was a large circle with the words "City of Milwaukee" on the top and "Wisconsin" on the bottom.

"How do you slide wearing that uniform?" I asked Mickey.

"It isn't easy, kid," she replied, lifting her dress to reveal a six-inch-long patch of reddened, scraped, and scabbed-over skin on her right thigh. "But if you want to play, you've got to pay."

Mickey wrapped some tape around the wounded leg and also around two of her fingers, which she said she had sprained in a collision at home plate during the last game. Then she strapped on her shin guards and chest protector. There was a knock at the door leading to the dugout.

"May I come in?" a man asked.

"It's Max," the tall blonde announced. The door was opened and a thin, older man came in. He was carrying a clipboard and wearing a regular baseball uniform, but with the Milwaukee Chicks logo on it.

"Good evening, Mr. Carey," the girls chanted respectfully.

"Who's he?" I whispered to Mickey.

"Max Carey," she replied. "Our manager."

"*The* Max Carey?" I asked in awe. "The Max Carey who played for the Pittsburgh Pirates?"

"Yup."

I knew all about Max Carey from my baseball books. He played twenty years in the majors and led the National League in steals ten times. And I was in the same room with him!

"Mr. Carey doesn't like mascots," Mickey whispered. "So keep your beak shut."

"Gather around, girls," Carey said, pulling up a chair to put his foot up on. Merle—who I couldn't stop staring at—turned off the radio, and all the players obediently clustered around Carey. I wasn't sure if I was supposed to be part of the discussion, so I hung back.

"We had the day off yesterday, thanks to President Roosevelt and General Eisenhower," Carey told the group. "We needed it. Girls, we're not hitting. Our bats are about as quiet as a busted clock. We've only won five games so far, against seven losses. That's not good. But it's still early. We can do better, and we will do better. Wisniewski?"

It was the very tall blonde who raised her hand. Now I knew her name. Connie Wisniewski. She was the one my little cousin idolized.

"Can you go nine innings tonight, Connie?" Carey asked.

"I think so, sir."

"I hope so," Carey continued. "A few of the girls

are sick today, and we're shorthanded. Everybody needs to pitch in and pull up the slack."

"I can pitch an inning if you need me," the serious girl with the glasses volunteered.

"Good, Doris. We're playing the Rockford Peaches again. We went over their lineup the other day, so I won't repeat myself now. You know what to expect. They're fast, they play hard, and they play aggressively."

"So do we, Coach!" another girl said. Except for Merle, she was the shortest one on the team.

"That's what I like to hear, Ziggy," Carey said. "This is a team sport. It's never *I*, it's always *we*. So let us all clasp hands."

The players formed a big circle around Max Carey.

"May this chain," he said, his head bowed, "with its golden links, its ideals and principles, carry us through to victory in the test just ahead and also through the years that are to come. Okay, let's get 'em!"

The players let out a whoop, grabbed their gloves, and charged out of the locker room in single file.

I realized this would be a good time for me to bail out of this situation. Clearly, I wasn't going to meet Mickey Mantle here. I had told my cousin I would be right back. It would be simple to take one of my new baseball cards, go sit in a quiet corner of the locker room, and send myself away from 1944 and back to my own time. Nobody was around. It would be easy. They'd never miss me.

On the other hand, not more than ten minutes before, I had seen the entire roster of the Milwaukee Chicks totally naked! Maybe I should stick around awhile.

I was mulling over this crucial decision when the voice of Max Carey echoed off the walls.

"Hey, you! Chicken!"

Being the only one dressed up as a chicken, I figured he had to be talking to me.

"Yes sir?"

"Take off that chicken head while I'm speaking to you."

Carefully, I removed my head.

"What's your name, sonny?"

"Joe Stoshack, sir."

"Oh yeah?" Carey sneered. "Any man who dresses up like a chicken is no man in my book. From now on, your name is Josephine. Is that clear?"

"Yes sir."

"What's your name?"

"Josephine, sir."

"Good," Carey said, staring me down. "I want you to know some things right from the start. I don't like mascots. Mascots are pathetic. This isn't Halloween. This is baseball. If people want to see puppets, they can go to a puppet show. If we have to have a giant chicken to bring in the fans, so be it.

But I don't have to like it . . . or you."

"Yes sir!"

"And another thing," Carey continued, "these girls are not here for your enjoyment, if you know what I mean. If I catch you fooling around with any of my players, you're out of here, buster. They are professional baseball players, and damn good ones. If they weren't, I wouldn't have come out of retirement to manage this team. Is that clear?"

"Yes sir!" I said, fighting to hide the smile that was threatening to appear on my face.

"Okay. Now go out there and do . . . whatever it is you do. Just stay out of my way and mind your p's and q's."

"Yes sir!"

I charged toward the door, but Carey wasn't quite done with me yet.

"Josephine!" he shouted. "Put your head on! Wear your full costume at all times on the field. That's league rules."

I attached the head and charged for the door again. Unfortunately, there was a pipe hanging down from the ceiling that, though higher than my head, was lower than the chicken's head. The pipe knocked the chicken head off mine and sent me sprawling to the locker room floor.

"Pathetic . . . ," Carey muttered, shaking his head and walking out the door.

6

A Real Chicken

IT GETS WARM AND MUGGY ON SUMMER NIGHTS IN
Milwaukee, especially when you're inside a giant
chicken suit. Fans were beginning to fill the bleachers at Borchert Field. The sweet smell of roasted
peanuts wafted through the stands.

"Red Cross blood donors will be admitted free at
tomorrow morning's game against the Racine
Belles," the public address announcer said. "Bring
your Red Cross button. Game time is ten o'clock."

"Hey, Chicken!" one of the fans hollered. "Buck,
buck, buck, buck!"

I had witnessed enough ball games to know the
responsibilities of a team mascot. You dance around
like an idiot. You pester the umpires and opposing
players. You entertain the fans and do everything you
can to keep them enthused. It's a humiliating,
degrading job, but somebody's got to do it.

I jumped on top of the Chicks dugout and proceeded to lead the crowd in a cheer.

"Gimme a C!" I shouted as loud as I could.

Nothing. Nobody responded. Silence.

"Gimme an H!"

Again, no response.

"Down in front!" yelled a bald, fat guy a few rows back.

"Yeah, we can't see!"

"Mommy, chicken is scary!" a little girl complained before bursting into tears.

People behind the dugout started to boo and throw ice cubes at me. I decided to cool it for a while and wait until the game started to drag before continuing my cheerleading efforts.

On the field, Max Carey was rapping out grounders to the Chicks infielders while the other team—the Rockford Peaches—played catch in the outfield.

The first thing I noticed—and this totally blew me away—was that these girls could throw! I had never seen a girl throw like a guy before. The girls in my league didn't seem to understand that when you throw a ball, your elbow is supposed to move forward first, and then you snap your hand forward from the elbow. But these girls were whipping the ball back and forth so fast and so skillfully, I could barely see it.

That was saying something, because the ball they were using was enormous. It looked even bigger than a softball. It was more like a small melon.

Then I noticed that the pitcher for the Chicks—Connie Wisniewski—was out of this world. The tallest player on the field, she would windmill her long right arm once, twice, sometimes three revolutions before releasing an underhand rocket toward home plate. She must have been throwing seventy or eighty miles per hour. The ball smacked into Mickey Maguire's mitt with a pop that could be heard all around the ballpark. It was a beautiful thing to see. I began to think that I might have to change my opinion about girls playing baseball.

Fans of all sorts were coming up to the front row railing to watch the players up close.

"Teeny!" an adoring little girl hollered. "Teeny Petras, can I have your autograph?"

"I like your curves, Connie!" an older guy hooted after sticking two fingers in his mouth to make a shrieking whistle. "Ain't she a beaut?"

"Marry me, Mickey!" shouted another guy.

"Thanks for the offer, bud," Mickey Maguire shot back with a laugh. "But I'm already married."

"If you got a husband," shouted a guy in a baseball cap who looked like he'd had one too many, "why ain'tcha home cookin' dinner for him?"

I turned to look at the heckler.

"Her husband is in Italy," I said, "fighting for your freedom."

"What do you know?" the guy replied. "You're

dressed up like a chicken!" The guys next to him, who looked just as drunk, laughed appreciatively.

"Let 'em razz me," Mickey told me. "I can handle myself."

"Oh, big girl," one of the drunks yelled sarcastically. "She can handle herself. A woman's place is at home!"

Mickey took off her mask and spit in the direction of the drunk guys. "Yeah, she said, "home *plate*."

"Next thing you know," the first guy said, "they'll have a monkey at short, a giraffe at third base, and a trained seal in center field!"

He and his friends thought that was brilliantly clever, and they congratulated themselves on their originality by clinking beers.

"Ah, blow it out your rear end," Mickey snorted, turning away from them to concentrate on Connie Wisniewski's fastballs.

I wondered about the men in the stands. If the able-bodied American men were fighting the war in Europe or the South Pacific, who were these guys? They must be too old to be drafted, too young, or have something wrong with them, I concluded. I noticed a few guys in Army uniforms who were missing legs. They were probably just back from the war.

I was staring into the crowd when a kid came down to the first row right in front of me. He was about my size and looked about my age, but he was smoking a cigarette.

"I'm here," he said to me. "You can take off the chicken suit."

"Huh?"

"What are you—deaf? I said take off the chicken suit. I'm the new mascot. Get the picture? Now wise up and take off the suit or I'll take it off for you."

I don't like being ordered around by kids, and I didn't like this kid's attitude. What was he going to do—jump over the fence and rip the chicken suit off me?

"You're late," I told him. "The early bird gets the worm, if you'll excuse the pun."

"Sez who?" the kid said. "They told me the job was mine!"

"Yeah, well, the next time somebody offers you a job, maybe you ought to think about showing up on time. They couldn't depend on you, so they hired me."

"That ain't fair!"

"Hey, life isn't always fair, pal," I said.

"I'm gonna get you but good."

Now he was getting me mad. I thought about throwing off the chicken head and showing him who was boss, but I didn't want to get in trouble with Max Carey.

"Ah, blow it out your rear end," I said, walking away from him.

I could feel my heart beating quickly as I walked across the field. Nothing gets my blood pumping better than the possibility of a fistfight.

I strolled over to Merle, who was playing catch with the girl Max Carey had called Ziggy. The more I looked at Merle, the more I liked what I saw.

"Hiya, Chicken!" she said. "What's cookin'?"

"Did you mean it before when you said I was cute?" I asked bashfully.

"Honey, you look good enough to eat!"

My heart beat even faster. She called me "honey"! She likes me! I realized for the first time that fighting was not the only way to get my blood pumping.

I was in love.

7

A Strike for Freedom

THE ROCKFORD PEACHES WERE FROM ROCKFORD, Illinois. They had peach-colored uniforms, of course, with reddish socks. As they took infield practice, they looked just as smooth as the Chicks.

Tiby Eisen getting her hair done. Now *there's* something you don't see at a big-league game!

In the Chicks dugout, the girls busied themselves in preparation for the game. Connie Wisniewski put a brace on her knee, which she had twisted the week before. Tiby Eisen, the peppy left fielder, braided her hair. She said she did it before every game for good luck. Mickey Maguire put more tape on her leg. First baseman Dolores Klosowski was peeling potatoes and dropping them into a bucket of water. Max Carey, apparently, believed that peeling potatoes strengthened the wrists. Either that or he really liked potatoes. I sat as close as I could to Merle, trying desperately to think of clever things to say to her.

After a while, a microphone stand was carried out and placed on home plate. When a priest walked out on the field, the Chicks stopped whatever they were doing and lined up along the first-base line. The Rockford Peaches did the same along the third-base line, so the two teams formed a giant V shape that met at home plate. All the players removed their caps and bowed their heads.

I wasn't sure if I was supposed to remove my chicken head or not. Max Carey had told me it was a league rule to keep it on, so I did.

"Will the crowd please rise," requested the public address announcer.

"Ladies and gentlemen," the priest spoke into the microphone, his words echoing around the ballpark, "as we sit here in the safety of Borchert Field, our sons, our brothers, our husbands, and our friends are at this moment fighting for their lives on the beaches of Normandy. Our nation did not start this fight. We didn't want to go to war. We fight this war because the most ambitious tyranny on earth has forced us to, and we would rather die fighting than live as slaves."

Some of the fans clapped and cheered respectfully.

"The next few days will be critical to all human history. Victory will not be easy, but it will come. Good always triumphs over evil."

More cheering and clapping arose from the stands.

"We can only pray," the priest continued. "We pray for the soldiers we know and also for the ones we don't. A few short years ago, they were all just young boys who needed our protection. Today, they protect us. We pray for them. We pray for ourselves too, who must face the dreadful waiting. And we pray for victory and a lasting peace. Amen."

The priest mumbled some words in another language, and the opening strains of the National Anthem blared out of the speakers. Behind me in the stands, a woman sobbed. When the song was over, the umpire, dressed in a black suit, hollered, "Play ball!"

The Chicks jogged back to the dugout and gathered around Max Carey.

"Keep your eyes and ears open," he advised. "Be unselfish, modest, humble, and cooperative. Win graciously and lose sportingly. Take the hard knocks as a matter of course, and blame none for your mistakes or shortcomings. Does everybody remember the signs?"

"You bet!"

"Good! Now let's show 'em what we're made of!"

The team whooped and ran out to their positions, with the home crowd cheering them on.

Connie Wisniewski whipped in a few warm-up

Merle
"The Blond Bombshell"
Keagle

Thelma
"Tiby"
Eisen

Betty
"Whitey"
Whiting

Ernestine
"Teeny"
Petras

Alma
"Ziggy"
Ziegler

Connie
"Iron Woman"
Wisniewski

Doris
"Tetz"
Tetzlaff

Dolores
"Lefty"
Klosowski

Dorothy
"Mickey"
Maguire

The positions of the Chicks.

pitches. The leadoff batter for the Peaches, a tall, skinny girl, watched carefully as if she was trying to figure out Connie's delivery. She tapped her bat against each cleat twice before stepping into the batter's box.

I thought about going into the stands to rile up the fans a little, but Max Carey glared at me, so I sat down. With the Chicks in the field, he and I were the only ones in the dugout.

"Come on, Iron Woman!" Mickey Maguire shouted from behind the plate. "Put it in here, you big tomato! Hmmm, baby! She couldn't hit you if she had a tennis racket!"

The game hadn't even begun yet, and Mickey's uniform was already smudged with dirt. She spit on her hand and wiped it on her dress.

"Strike one!"

The pitch came in so fast, I didn't even see it. I just heard a hissing sound as the ball crossed home plate.

"Thatababy!" shouted Mickey. "Now give her your rise ball. Let's see the old slingshot, Connie!"

The batter stepped out. She may not have seen the first pitch either. When she got back into the batter's box, she had choked up on the bat and was crouching down. It was obvious that she was trying to make her strike zone smaller.

Connie windmilled her arm three times and let the ball fly. The pitch was a little high.

"Ball one!" called the ump.

Connie windmilled her arm three times and let the ball fly.

"Good eye!" somebody called from the Peaches bench. "Wait for a good one."

"Give her your wrinkle now, Connie," shouted Mickey. "She can't hit the curve even if she knows it's coming!"

Balls two and three followed, much to the dismay of Connie Wisniewski. Mickey whipped the ball back to Connie hard, like she wanted to shake her up. When the ump called the next pitch ball four, Mickey wheeled around and flung off her mask.

"Listen, you dim-witted blockhead!" she hollered at the umpire. "If you'd stop staring at the batter's legs for a minute, you might see some strikes!"

"I ain't starin' at her legs," the ump shot back in Mickey's face, "and if you don't shut up, you'll be staring at the inside of the locker room!"

Mickey laughed and put her mask back on. The batter jogged to first. She did have nice legs.

The times I've played softball, there was no stealing bases, and runners were not even allowed to take a lead until after the pitch crossed the plate. But the runner on first danced off the bag right away and took off for second on the first pitch to the next batter.

Mickey caught the pitch and gunned it on a line to Ziggy Ziegler, playing second base. The runner slid in along with a cloud of dust. The plate umpire was the only umpire, so he made the call.

"Safe!"

"We had her by a mile!" Mickey hollered.

"I said *safe*," asserted the ump.

"Ah, you're blind as a bat!" Mickey complained.

"I'm warning you, Maguire! One more word and I'll throw you outta here!"

Max Carey whistled for Mickey to come over.

"Mick," he said, sweeping his arm across the

dugout. "I don't have any subs. We can't afford for you to get ejected from this game."

"I'm just fooling with him, Max," Mickey said. "If I kick and scream about the close ones now, maybe he'll give us a break when we need one later." She threw him a wink before taking her position behind the plate again.

"Smack one outta here, Mildred!" somebody hollered from the other dugout as the next batter stepped up.

Mildred was a big girl, maybe even fat. But Connie Wisniewski wasn't intimidated. She blew three fastballs by her, with the runner stealing third on the strikeout. Mickey's throw was off line and she let out a curse. One out, runner on third.

It occurred to me that the game they were playing wasn't quite baseball, but it wasn't softball either. It was something in the middle. There was base stealing, and nine fielders, like in baseball. But the pitching was underhand, with a very large ball, as in softball. And when somebody hit a foul ball into the crowd, the fans threw the ball back onto the field.

The number-four batter for the Peaches stepped up. Max Carey waved for the outfield to move back a few steps, and I knew why. Managers always put their strongest power hitter in the number-four slot. That way, if the first three hitters get on, the cleanup batter might clear the fence and clear the bases.

This cleanup hitter didn't clear anything, though. She tapped a little dribbler to the right side of the diamond. Connie rushed off the pitcher's mound, but she was moving slowly because of her bad leg. Ziggy couldn't get there in time from her position at second base. The runner was safe at first. The runner at third stayed there.

In the dugout, Max Carey didn't curse or throw anything. He began to relay a series of signs to Mickey and the Chicks infielders. He touched the bill of his cap, stroked his elbow with the other hand, and wiped his hand across his chest.

"Watch for the double steal!" a fan shouted.

The manager of the Peaches was flashing signs back and forth with his base runners too. Something was up. The next Peach stepped into the batter's box.

On the first pitch, the batter swung and missed. The Peach runner took off from first. Mickey made the throw, but she didn't throw down to second. She whipped the ball right back to Connie on the pitcher's mound. The runner at third had taken a few steps toward home. Connie whirled around and pegged the ball to third. The runner was dead. She didn't even get back to the bag.

"Yer out!" called the ump. The hometown fans roared in approval.

"Ha-ha-ha!" Max Carey clapped his hands. "I love that play."

The Peach who had been picked off third slinked back to her dugout in shame. Flustered, the batter popped the next pitch up to Merle—the love of my life—in center field for the third out, and the Chicks dashed off the field.

"Beautiful!" Carey cheered as the players filled the dugout.

"That was a nice catch you made," I told Merle as I slid next to her on the bench.

"It was nothin', darlin'."

She called me "darlin'"! So far she had said I was cute, she called me "snookums," "honey," and now "darlin'." I was in heaven. Trying my best to make small talk with her, I almost missed the public address announcement.

"Ladies and gentlemen, please direct your attention to the home plate area, where the Milwaukee Chicken will throw a strike for freedom!"

"I think they're callin' you, sweetie."

She called me "sweetie"!

"Get on the field, Josephine!" barked Max Carey.

Two burly guys were carrying a piece of plywood that was about ten feet tall and five feet wide, with a hole in the middle about the size of a poster. When they turned the plywood over and stood it up on home plate, I could see there was a cartoony painting of a goofily grinning Adolf Hitler on it. The hole in the board was where one of Hitler's teeth should have been.

"If Chicken can throw a ball through Hitler's

tooth," boomed the announcer, "he will be throwing a strike for freedom!"

"Nobody told me I would have to throw a ball," I complained, shrinking back into the dugout.

"Get out there," Mickey said as she and the rest of the team grabbed me and pushed me out of the dugout, "and quit your bellyaching!"

The two burly guys—each of them had a name tag that said BOB on it —took me by my wings and half led, half dragged me out to the mound. One of the Bobs flipped me a ball. I kept shaking my chicken head.

"What are you, chicken?" a fan yelled, to the amusement of the crowd. That got the rest of them going, and in seconds the whole place was either jeering or cheering for me.

"Just to make things interesting," the announcer said, "if Chicken throws the ball through Hitler's tooth, each and every man, woman, and child in the ballpark tonight will receive a free pass to see Judy Garland in *Meet Me in St. Louis,* now playing in air-conditioned splendor at the Palace Theater on Wisconsin Avenue."

"Oooooooooooooooooooh!"

"B-but I need a warm-up," I protested. "I haven't practiced."

"Shut up and throw," one of the Bobs said. "We ain't got all night."

"Yeah," said the other Bob, "and you better throw it through the hole, Chicken, 'cause I really want to see that picture."

I toed the rubber and fingered the huge ball, doing my best to wrap my hand around it. I've always had a pretty good arm, but I wasn't used to this kind of pressure. At our Little League games, usually only the moms and dads showed up. There must have been four or five thousand people watching me.

"You better not miss, Chicken!" somebody yelled.

"If he does, let's fry him!"

"You can do it, sweetie pie!" Merle shouted from the Chicks dugout. "Concentrate."

I looked over at her. She had her hands clasped together, like she was praying. Man, she was beautiful. I wanted to throw the strike just for her.

Right above Merle, in the third row behind the Chicks dugout, I spotted that kid who had shown up for the mascot job. He was giving me a dirty look.

The crowd began to clap their hands and stamp their feet in rhythm.

I gripped the ball and concentrated on Hitler's face. I took a deep breath. It was hard to do a regular windup with the chicken suit on, but I did the best I could. As I let go of the ball, my forward momentum almost caused the chicken head to fall off.

The ball sailed two feet over Hitler's head. The crowd let out a groan.

"Ohhhhh!" moaned the announcer. "Too bad, Chicken! Maybe next time!"

"Booooooooooooooooo!"

"He's a bum!"

"Get a new chicken!"

"Kill the chicken!"

I ran off the field, dodging lemons, bottles, and other junk that came flying out of the stands. Luckily, I made it back to the Chicks dugout with only a few small objects hitting me.

Connie, Merle, Mickey, and Tiby told me to forget about it. They said that hardly anyone can throw very accurately under the circumstances. Max Carey just looked at me.

"Pathetic," he muttered. "Just pathetic."

Trick Play

IN THE BOTTOM OF THE FIRST INNING, THE CHICKS offense exploded. A clean single, an infield hit, and an error loaded the bases for Mickey, who delivered with a double in the gap to drive in all three runs.

Dolores Klosowski got a double too, and Ziggy singled her home. Connie Wisniewski poked a grounder through the infield.

By then, the fans were going crazy. When Teeny Petras got hit by a pitch, they started booing. The manager of the Peaches came out to protest that the ball had hit Teeny's bat, but she held up her left arm to show that the seams of the ball had made an impression in her skin. The umpire waved her to first. Tiby Eisen got hit too, on the hand. Max Carey made a quick splint out of two Popsicle sticks supplied by some fans, and Tiby stayed in the game.

The only bad thing that happened to the Chicks

Mickey taking a cut.

was that third baseman Doris Tetzlaff got called back to the dugout by the umpire and fined five dollars because she had forgotten to put lipstick on.

When the inning was over, the Chicks had batted around and pushed six runs across the plate.

"You're our good luck charm, sweetie pie!" Merle said as the Chicks piled into the dugout. Max Carey shot me a puzzled look and I just shrugged.

"I didn't do anything," I said.

"Well, keep not doing anything," he replied. "Whatever you're not doing, it's working."

In the second inning, the Peaches put runners on second and third with two outs. But the runner on second was taking a very long lead, so Mickey called for a pitchout and picked her off.

Chicks 6, Peaches 0.

The innings went by and Connie Wisniewski was cruising. The Peaches were baffled by her pitches, which appeared to rise and curve at the same time.

After each side was retired, there was some sort of promotion for the crowd. In the second inning, the Milwaukee Fire Department drove their new pumper out on the field, to the applause of the fans. In the third inning, there was a dog obedience demonstration. Two random fans were awarded a bag of groceries and an electric roaster in the fourth inning. Through it all, vendors circulated around the stands, selling not just hot dogs but also war bonds, to support the troops fighting overseas.

By the fourth inning, the sun was gone and the lights—not nearly as bright as the outdoor lights I had seen in the twenty-first century—were turned on. Swarms of insects that had been buzzing around the field took turns flying suicide missions into the hot bulbs.

The Peaches had squeezed out a couple of runs by that time, so the score was 6-2 when the Chicks came to bat in the bottom of the fourth. Mickey was swinging a bat in the on-deck circle.

"Ladies and gentlemen," the public address announcer said, "an important news bulletin has just come over the wires from Europe."

Everyone in the ballpark—even the hot dog

vendors—stopped what they were doing.

"We have just received word that the Allies have captured the city of Rome. I repeat, the capital of Italy has fallen to the Allies! On to Berlin and Tokyo!"

A roar swept across the crowd. People were hugging each other and throwing their hats in the air.

I didn't know that much about World War II, but I did know we fought against Germany, Italy, and Japan. I knew that the war ended when we dropped atomic bombs on Japan. If Rome had been defeated and the D day invasion had begun, that meant we were winning the war.

Everybody in the Chicks dugout was happy about the news. Then I noticed Mickey in the on-deck circle. She wasn't swinging her bat back and forth anymore. She was just standing there, as if she was frozen.

Then I remembered. Her husband was fighting in Italy. His rhyme had stuck in my head—"When the Allies take Rome, I'm coming home." After being apart for two years, Mickey and her husband would finally be together again.

One by one, the other Chicks noticed Mickey, standing like a statue in the on-deck circle. I waited for a big smile to break out across her face, but it didn't come. She looked very serious, like she was deep in thought.

"Didja hear that, Mick?" Tiby Eisen bubbled, running out of the dugout to give her a hug.

"Tom's coming home!"

Mickey hugged Tiby for a few seconds. Then she spit and wiped her hands on her dress as she went up to home plate.

"I heard it," she said. "Let's play ball."

The Chicks were silent, shooting puzzled looks and shrugged shoulders at each other.

"What's with her?" I asked Merle.

"Beats me."

After she grounded to short and sat back on the bench, nobody said a word to Mickey. She didn't look like she wanted to talk about it. It was like the announcement had never been made.

Dolores Klosowski went back to peeling her potatoes. Max Carey went back to flashing signs and barking encouragement. I went back to flirting with Merle.

Then in the top of the fifth inning, Connie Wisniewski's fastball must have lost a few miles per hour, because the Peaches suddenly started hitting. After a pair of singles, a passed ball, and a triple, the score was 6-5, and the Peaches looked like they were about to break the game wide open. They had runners at second and third with their cleanup batter—a lefty—strolling to the plate.

"Two outs, girls!" shouted Max Carey. "We need an out, bad."

Mickey asked the umpire for time out, and she came rushing to the dugout.

"You okay, Mick?" Carey asked her.

"Yeah, I'm fine. Flip me one of those potatoes, will you, Stosh?"

I grabbed a potato out of the bucket on the ground near the end of the Chicks bench and tossed it to her.

"Why do you need a potato at a time like this?" Carey asked.

"You'll see," Mickey said, slipping the potato inside her chest protector and going back behind the plate.

Connie looked in for the sign. The batter pumped her bat back and forth slowly. The infielders got ready. The runners danced off second and third.

"Come on, Connie babe!" Mickey hollered. "Put it in here."

Mickey's sign must have been for a pitchout. As soon as Connie let go of the ball, Mickey jumped to the left of the plate. The pitchout was right where she wanted it. She grabbed it and whipped it to third.

Or, I thought she whipped it to third, anyway. What she had actually done was catch the ball, take the potato out from behind her chest protector, and whip the potato to third.

Not that anybody in the ballpark knew that at the time. It looked like a baseball.

Doris Tetzlaff, playing third, reached for the pickoff throw, but it was way too high. The potato sailed into left field.

Mickey Maguire behind the plate.

The runner on third base saw the errant pickoff, clapped her hands gleefully, and trotted home with what she thought was the tying run.

Mickey, however, was standing in front of the plate with the ball in her hand. She calmly tagged out the runner, who had a look on her face like she had seen a ghost.

"Yer out!" cried the umpire. Then he stopped. "Hold everything! What'd she throw?"

One of the Peaches ran out to left field to

retrieve the unidentified flying object.

"It's a potato!" she screamed, jogging back to show the evidence to the umpire.

"So what?" Mickey said. "It's not my fault if she's so dumb she can't tell the difference between a baseball and a potato."

"You can't throw a potato!" the umpire yelled at Mickey.

"Why not?"

"It's against the rules!"

"Show me where it says in the rule book that throwing a potato is illegal," Mickey challenged.

"A potato is a foreign object!"

"It is not," Mickey claimed. "It's from Idaho!"

In seconds, both teams were crowding around home plate, yelling, kicking dirt at the umpire, and shoving each other. Fruit and vegetables of all sorts were thrown on the field by the fans, who, for the most part, considered the potato incident amusing. I grabbed a few more potatoes out of the bucket and tossed them to the fans in the front row for the fun of it.

It took fifteen minutes before the ump was able to restore order. In the end, he ruled that Mickey had interfered with play, and the runner was safe at home.

At the end of five innings, it was Chicks 6, Peaches 6.

9

The All-American Girl

NEITHER TEAM SCORED OVER THE NEXT THREE INNINGS, and it was still a tie game when the Chicks came to bat in the bottom of the ninth. I had been playing patty-cake with some little kids in the stands, but returned to the dugout in time to watch the game.

Chicks first baseman Dolores Klosowski was the leadoff batter. She was a lefty, and the Peach defense shifted to the right accordingly.

With the count at 2-2, Dolores slapped a grounder to the left side of the infield. The third baseman bobbled the ball for a moment. Dolores, seeing she had a chance to make it to first safely, lunged for the bag as the first baseman reached for the throw.

Her left foot slipped as she touched first, and Dolores tried to brace herself with her other leg. But she was moving too fast. I could see her leg was bent at a weird angle as she tumbled in a heap just past first base. There was a sick-sounding crack.

"Safe!" called the ump.

"Owwwww!" Dolores cried, writhing on the ground, holding her leg.

We all rushed out of the Chicks dugout behind Max Carey, who had picked up the first aid kit the instant Dolores hit the dirt.

"Give her room!" he screamed. "Call a doctor! Her leg may be broken."

Dolores was on her side, tears and makeup streaming down her face. The umpire looked on with sympathy.

"If it's dislocated, I know how to snap it back in place," Connie volunteered.

"Touch that leg and you're dead!" Dolores shouted through the pain.

"Get a stretcher," Max Carey ordered, "and an ambulance. That bone is broken."

The Chicks carried Dolores back to the locker room. The ump gave Carey a five-minute injury time-out. In the distance, an ambulance siren was already wailing. A couple of the girls held Dolores's hands and tried to comfort her.

"Who's gonna play first base in the tenth inning?" Mickey asked Max Carey.

"If we can score a run," he replied, "we won't need a first baseman. There won't be a tenth inning."

"Yeah, but we need a pinch runner for Dolores right now."

Max Carey looked around the locker room. He

had used all his players. His gaze fell on me.

"Hey, Josephine," he said. "Can you run fast?"

"Yeah," I replied.

"You know how to slide?"

"Sure. Why?"

"I want you to go in there and run for Dolores."

"What are you, crazy?" I said, backing into the corner. "I'm a guy."

"So what?" Mickey said. "You don't have to hit. You don't have to play the field. Just run the bases. Don't worry, we'll drive you in."

"Th-this is ridiculous!" I stammered. "Everyone will know right away I'm not a girl."

"No they won't," Mickey insisted. "I've got an extra uniform. We're about the same size. With a cap on—"

"I'm not putting on a dress!" I protested.

"It's not a dress," Connie informed me. "It's a skirt."

I wasn't sure what was the difference between a dress and a skirt. But I knew they were both worn by women, and there was no way I was going to put on women's clothes.

"Male bagpipers wear skirts all the time," Doris Tetzlaff pointed out.

"I don't play bagpipes!" I shouted.

"Don't be such a baby," Tiby said. "Look, you already dressed up like a chicken. What's the big deal?"

"We don't have anyone else," Max Carey said. "If we don't produce a pinch runner in three minutes, we have to forfeit the game, girls."

All of them looked at me, with big eyes and pleading puppy dog faces.

"I won't do it!" I insisted. "And that's final!"

"Come on, be a man about it," Mickey pleaded. "Put on the skirt."

That's when they grabbed me. The entire team—with the exception of Dolores Klosowski, who was being loaded into an ambulance—attacked me. I was helpless. They were all over me, pulling off the chicken suit and ripping off my shirt and pants.

"Help!" I screamed. "Give me back my clothes!"

"We should really shave his legs!" Ziggy hollered. "He's pretty hairy."

"No time for that!" Mickey replied.

Once they had me down to my underwear, four of the Chicks held my arms and legs while the rest of them put the dress or skirt or whatever it was on me. I struggled to get free, but they were too strong. Tiby and Teeny put a pair of cleats on my feet, and Ziggy stuffed a couple of balled-up pairs of sweat socks in the front of the uniform.

"There," Mickey declared as she put a Chicks cap on my head. "Nobody will know you're a guy."

"You look spiffy, sugar!" Merle said.

"This is embarrassing," I whined.

"I don't know," Tiby said, looking me up and down. "I think he needs a little makeup."

"No makeup!" I shouted. "Even guys who play bagpipes don't wear makeup!"

"Lipstick at the very least," Tiby decided.

"No!"

They grabbed me again before I could make a run for it. Five or six of them pinned me to the floor while Tiby ran to get her makeup case.

"It's a five-dollar fine if you get caught without lipstick on," Mickey said. "You don't want to get fined, do you?"

This was all my stupid cousin's fault. If she hadn't slipped the Mickey Maguire card in place of my Mickey Mantle card, this never would have happened. I could be partying with Mickey Mantle right now instead of being tortured and humiliated by these lunatic girls.

"Will you stop wriggling around?" Tiby said as she painted my lips. "I'm gonna smear it all over your face!"

"Stop dillydallying!" shouted Max Carey, who was on his way to the dugout to confer with the umpire. "Step on it, girls!"

When they were done with my makeover, they let me off the floor.

"You look like a real all-American girl now," Mickey said as she led me to the dugout, like a prisoner on his way to jail.

"Pinch running for Klosowski," boomed the public address announcer, "Josephine Stoshack."

Max Carey looked me up and down, then shook his head.

"Pathetic," he grumbled. "Simply pathetic."

It took the whole team to push me out of the dugout and onto the field.

10

Pinch Runner

I'VE HAD A FEW HUMILIATING EXPERIENCES IN MY LIFE. Like the time my pants fell down while we were climbing the ropes in gym class. And then there was the time I claimed I could balance on one edge of a canoe on Hopkins Pond. But this, by far, topped them all.

I jogged out to first base, pulling my cap down low in hopes that it wouldn't be so obvious that I was a guy. Mickey was coaching first base. Max Carey had come out of the dugout to coach third.

"Okay, listen carefully," Mickey instructed. "There are no outs. If the ball is hit in the air, you've got to return to first. On the ground, you've got to go."

"I know all that—"

"Not so low!" Mickey warned me. "They'll hear you!"

"I know all that," I repeated, raising my voice to

sound like a girl. "I've been in Little League for five years."

"Wait!" Mickey whispered as she peered into the dugout. "Max is giving you the steal sign."

"What?" I complained. "Max isn't even in the dugout. I don't want to steal. I thought you said you guys would drive me in."

"No time to argue. Max is the manager. He's relaying the signs from third. He's trying to stay out of a double play situation. You're stealing on the first pitch. If you make it safely, watch the dugout. If Tiby flips her pigtails, that means you steal third. Got it?"

"Uh, yeah," I replied. "Tiby is the one with glasses and blond hair, right?"

"Yeah. And if you see her sign, you let Max know by touching the hem of your skirt."

"What's a hem?"

"The bottom part."

"Okay."

This was complicated. Until this season, the "steal" sign of my Little League team was when one of the coaches shouted "Steal!"

Betty Whiting, the Chicks right fielder, was up. I took a few short steps off first base, keeping an eye on the pitcher. She was watching me out of the corner of her eye. I wanted to get a good jump, but I had to be careful not to get too far off first or I'd get picked off.

"Strike her out!" the catcher hollered. "No

batter. No batter."

The pitcher went into her windup and I took off. Betty swung and missed, which served to prevent the catcher from charging forward to make the throw to second.

I dug my cleats into the hard infield dirt, pumping my legs as fast as I could move them. The Peaches shortstop was coming over to take the throw. The stupid skirt was getting in the way of my legs as I ran. Five feet from the bag, I hit the dirt, hooking my toe around the right side of the base just like Coach Tropiano had taught me. I held a hand to my head to prevent my cap from flying off. The shortstop caught the ball on a hop and slapped the tag on my leg.

"Safe!" called the umpire, who had run out from behind the plate.

The players in the Chicks dugout were on their feet, screaming for me. I got up and dusted the dirt off my skirt.

"Way to go, Josephine!" Mickey hollered.

"Thatagirl!"

Standing on second base, I took a moment to catch my breath and make sure the shortstop threw the ball back to the pitcher. I didn't want her to pull the old "hidden ball" trick on me.

"You must be new," the shortstop said to me.

"Yeah," I said in a fake high voice. "This is my first game."

"Say, a bunch of us are going dancing tonight,"

she said. "Wanna come?"

"I can't," I replied. "I'm . . . uh . . . getting my hair done." Girls are always getting their hair done, I figured.

"Really? Are you getting a perm? You'd look good with a perm."

"Yeah," I agreed, "a perm."

I didn't know what a perm was, but I seemed to remember my mom got one once. She came home and her hair was all curly. She looked like Little Orphan Annie.

"Josephine!" Max Carey shouted from the third-base coaching box. "Stop squawking and get your head in the game!"

I looked to the dugout. Tiby was frantically flipping her pigtails. That meant Max wanted me to steal third! I touched the hem of my skirt to let him know I had seen the sign.

"Good luck with your perm." The shortstop giggled. I had the feeling that she had only been trying to distract me by talking about my hair.

By stealing second base, I had made it so that the Peaches could not get a double play or even a force-out on a ground ball. There was no pressure to steal third on the next pitch, so I just watched Betty take it for a called strike two. She swung and missed at the next one. One out.

Ziggy was up next. I didn't know if she was a good hitter, but she was waving her bat around menacingly. She watched two pitches out of the strike zone. I figured if I stayed close to second base, the Peaches pitcher might not think I was a threat to steal third and she wouldn't pay such close attention to me.

It's harder to steal third base than it is to steal second, because the distance from the catcher is much shorter. I knew I would need to get a really big jump on the pitcher.

The shortstop wasn't holding me on, so I got a good walking lead off the base. As soon as the pitcher windmilled her arm, I dug for third.

The element of surprise gave me a slight advantage. The third baseman rushed to the bag to get into position for the throw. Max Carey, coaching third, put his hands down, the classic "slide" sign.

I remembered reading in one of my baseball books at home that Ty Cobb used to look at the infielder's eyes while he slid into the base. The eyes told him where the ball was going. Then he would either slide his toe into the opposite side of the base or stick his toe in the path of the ball and try to kick it away.

I tried to do that too. I ran all out, and while the third baseman waited for the throw, I slid in and stuck my foot into her glove. The ball hit my cleat and bounced away. She let out a curse.

"Safe!" hollered the ump.

The Chicks were screaming and cheering in the dugout. Max Carey came over to me as I dusted off my skirt. I was gasping for breath.

"Okay, good," he said. "Now listen. You've got to use your noodle now. There's one out. You're not forced to run. Don't do anything stupid like try to steal home. Give Ziggy the chance to drive you in. If she gets a hit, you're home and we win. If she hits a fly ball to the outfield, you tag up and we win. A passed ball or wild pitch, you slide in and we win. But if she hits a grounder or infield pop, you stay put. Got it?"

"Got it."

The count on Ziggy was 2-1. A good hitter's count. Ziggy waved her bat around. She looked like she really wanted to get the game-winning hit.

Maybe too much. She popped the ball up. I dashed back to third. The first baseman grabbed the pop for the second out. Disgusted with herself, Ziggy trudged back to the dugout. Connie Wisniewski stepped up to the plate.

"C'mere," Max Carey said to me. Then he whispered in my ear, "Steal home."

"What?!" I replied. "Steal home? A minute ago, you told me not to do anything stupid like steal home!"

"That was a minute ago," Max explained. "There was only one out then, and Ziggy is a good hitter. But now there are two outs. Connie is our last hope to drive you in. If she makes an out here, we have to go to extra innings. Connie has a bum knee, and she's not swinging the bat well. So you've got to drive yourself in."

"But—"

"Steal home," Carey hissed in my ear.

You hardly ever see anybody steal home in a baseball game. There's a good reason for that. It's almost impossible. A thrown ball moves faster than even the fastest runner. To steal home, you have to get a great jump, a tough pitch for the catcher to handle, and a certain amount of luck.

But if Max wanted me to go for it, I would. I took a deep breath and waited while Connie pumped her bat slowly.

"Get a hit, Connie!" somebody shouted from the stands.

"You can do it!"

I edged off third. The third baseman was a few steps in front of me, in case Connie tried to squeeze me home with a bunt. The pitcher glared at me. I wasn't going to wait for her to wind up. As soon as she turned her head back to the plate, I took off.

"She's going!" the catcher screamed.

I made a run for the plate like somebody had planted a bomb in third base. The pitcher rushed her delivery. Connie backed away from the plate to give me room to slide.

Watching the catcher's eyes, I could tell the ball was going to get home before I would. She moved forward to block the plate.

Just when I was about to slide, I saw the ball was already in her mitt. I was dead. My only hope was to go in standing up and knock the ball loose.

I put my head down and arms over my face to give me at least a little protection. It was going to be a nasty collision, I knew that for sure.

I crashed into the catcher without slowing down. Together we tumbled to the ground, all arms and legs. I fell heavily on home plate, having no idea if I was safe, out, or maybe even thrown out of the game for unneccesary roughness. I was exhausted from running the bases. There was a sharp pain in my back.

I looked up for the umpire's call, but he hadn't given it yet. He was looking to see if the catcher was holding the ball.

Something was jabbing into my back, so I rolled over to get off it.

It was the ball.

"Safe!" the umpire shouted.

The fans went nuts. The Chicks were out of the dugout before I could get up, shrieking with delight. They mobbed me, hugging me, kissing me, pounding me on the back. Max Carey told me I had "moxie." I didn't know what moxie was, but I figured it had to be something good, and I was glad I had it.

Final score: Chicks 7, Peaches 6.

And I, Josephine Stoshack, was the hero.

11

Play Like Men, Look Like Girls

THE GAME WAS OVER, THE CHICKS HAD WON, AND EVERY-
body was happy. As we piled triumphantly into the
dugout, I had one thing on my mind— there was an
excellent chance that I would get to see the Chicks
naked again.

I'm not proud of it or anything. I know I should
have been thinking about how I had contributed to
the victory. I should have been thinking about
Dolores Klosowski and her broken leg. My dad in
the hospital back home. But I'm being honest here.
I'm thirteen years old. I don't know about you, but I
know what I think about pretty much all the time.

In fact, I had been thinking about it ever since
they held me down and forced me to put on a dress.
Right then and there, it had occurred to me that
after the game I'd be in the locker room again. If I
could just blend into the woodwork, they just might

forget I was there.

"P.K. is coming!" Tiby shouted just as we entered the locker room.

"He's probably going to congratulate us on our stirring victory!" Ziggy beamed.

"Quick! Clean up the mess!" Connie shouted. "P.K. hates a sloppy locker room!"

The girls started running back and forth, throwing things into lockers, drawers, and cabinets. Nobody was taking any clothes off.

"Who's P.K.?" I asked Mickey Maguire.

"Philip K. Wrigley," she replied. "You know, the chewing gum guy. He owns the Cubs."

Of course, I'd had Wrigley gum. I had even been to Wrigley Field in Chicago. But why was Philip K. Wrigley coming here?

"He owns our whole league," Mickey informed me. She said Wrigley started the All-American Girls Professional Baseball League because he was afraid the war might completely shut down baseball. With so many major and minor leaguers away fighting, there would be a lot of empty ballparks.

According to Mickey, P.K. was a little odd. He wouldn't dial the telephone, for instance. His wife dialed for him. He was a millionaire, but he rode a motorcycle to work. And he once paid a guy five thousand dollars to put a hex on the Cubs' opponents.

The girls had just about finished tidying up the locker room when a voice boomed down the hallway.

"If the boys in the lab can't create a chewing gum that doesn't stick to false teeth, then tell 'em to create false teeth that don't stick to chewing gum! Get on it, Tommy!"

"Yes, P.K.," answered some other guy.

Suddenly, two men burst into the locker room. The older, grayer one was clearly Mr. Wrigley. The other one was short, geeky, and had the look of a low-paid, pencil-pushing yes-man. Each man wore a suit and a hat and carried a briefcase. I looked around for Max Carey, but he must have left already.

Suddenly, two men burst into the locker room. The older, grayer one was clearly Mr. Wrigley.

"Oops!" Wrigley said, as if he had entered the locker room by accident. He covered his eyes with his hand. "Is everybody decent?"

"Good evening, Mr. Wrigley," the girls replied sweetly.

"Evening, girls. Who wants gum?"

"I do!" everyone declared enthusiastically, and the guy named Tommy passed out gum all around.

"I have some exciting news, girls!" Wrigley announced. "I just signed a contract with the Milwaukee Symphony! They're going to entertain the fans before each game in the second half of the season! In tuxedos! Isn't that great?"

Why, I asked myself, *would baseball fans want to listen to classical music before a game?* Looking around the room at the blank faces, it appeared that the players were asking themselves the same question.

"That's fabulous, Mr. Wrigley," Mickey said, not very convincingly.

"Yeah, maybe we'll be inspired to play better after hearing some Beethoven and Mozart and stuff," Tiby cracked, hiding a smirk.

I'm not sure if Wrigley caught the sarcasm, but his mood seemed to change after Tiby's remark.

"Sit down, girls," he said quietly. He didn't continue until everyone was seated. "I started this league a year ago to help take people's minds off the war for a few hours every day. That's our main job. Those people in the stands, their sons and husbands and boyfriends are living in foxholes; they're getting shot at, bombed, injured, and killed. We want them to forget about that for just a little while."

"We're doing our best, Mr. Wrigley," Ziggy said.

"I know," Wrigley went on. "But we've got to do better. I don't need to tell you there are a lot of empty seats out there every game. You see them. We need to put fannies in those bleachers if this team and this league are going to be successful."

"What are you planning to do, Mr. Wrigley?" Mickey asked, almost meekly.

"Tommy and I have batted around a bunch of ideas," Wrigley said, gesturing to his assistant. "I have an important meeting to get to, so I'm going to let Tommy go over the details with you."

Tommy the geek went to the center of the locker room while Wrigley made his way toward the door.

"Oh, one last thing," Wrigley said before leaving, "I love the new chicken."

Everybody smiled at me as Tommy the geek took off his suit jacket and hat, pulled a notebook out of his briefcase, and cleared his throat. With his boss out of the room, Tommy seemed to enjoy being in charge.

"Girls, I'm going to give you the straight skinny," Tommy announced. "Mr. Wrigley didn't like what he saw out there tonight. Arguments with the umpire. Yelling at the fans. Being called back to the dugout to put on your lipstick. Potatoes being thrown on the field! You girls have to shape up. It's just not ladylike."

"Baseball isn't ladylike," Ziggy muttered, loud enough to be heard by everyone.

"Look," Tommy said, putting down his notebook, "nobody wants to see tomboys play baseball. The attraction is that you are girls. That is what is entertaining. To attract fans—especially male fans—you've got to look and act more like girls."

"And what, exactly, do girls look and act like?" Mickey asked, her hands on her hips.

"Girls are feminine," Tommy stated firmly. "That means lipstick, nail polish, and makeup on at all times. Hair stylishly groomed. Courteous and polite language. You should walk, talk, and behave like ladies."

"So in other words," Connie Wisniewski said, "you want us to play like men, but look like girls."

"Exactly!" Tommy exclaimed. "You see, men don't want to come out to the ballpark and see women who look like men."

"Are you saying we look like men?" Mickey said, taking one step toward Tommy.

"I didn't say that," Tommy replied, shrinking backward and holding his briefcase over his chest.

"Sure you did."

"What difference does it make what we look like?" Ziggy asked. "I thought we were here to win ball games."

"You are," Tommy agreed. "But let me set you straight. You are entertainers first and ballplayers second. Don't forget that."

"Well, as long as we have our priorities straight," Tiby snorted.

"Just in case some of you didn't read our league's rules of conduct, Mr. Wrigley requested that I post them for all to see." Tommy pulled a sheet of paper out of his briefcase and tacked it up on the bulletin board.

RULES OF CONDUCT

1. ALWAYS appear in feminine attire. AT NO TIME MAY A PLAYER APPEAR IN THE STANDS IN HER UNIFORM OR WEAR SLACKS OR SHORTS IN PUBLIC.

2. Boyish bobs are not permissible, and your hair should be well groomed at all times with longer hair preferable to short haircuts. Lipstick should always be worn.

3. Smoking or drinking is not permissible in public places. Obscene language will not be allowed at any time.

4. All public social engagements must be approved.

5. All living quarters and eating facilities must be approved. No player shall change her residence without permission.

6. All players must be in their rooms two hours after the finish of each game.

7. Baseball uniform skirts shall not be shorter than six inches above the kneecap.

8. The members of different teams must not socialize at any time during the season.

9. Players are not allowed to drive their cars past the city limits without the special permission of their manager.

FINES OF FIVE DOLLARS FOR THE FIRST OFFENSE, TEN DOLLARS FOR SECOND, AND SUSPENSION FOR THIRD WILL AUTOMATICALLY BE IMPOSED FOR BREAKING ANY OF THE ABOVE RULES.

"What?"

"You've got to be kidding!"

"Ten bucks?"

"You're going to tell us where we're allowed to eat?"

"You're going to tell us where we're allowed to drive?"

The Chicks were in open rebellion. I was afraid they were going to take the rules of conduct list right off the bulletin board and rip it up.

"Girls! Girls!" Tommy shouted, raising his voice and his hands to get their attention. "Simmer down. If attendance doesn't go up, Mr. Wrigley is going to move the Chicks away from Milwaukee next season."

"We've only played thirteen games!" Mickey said. "Give us a chance."

"We like it here," insisted Ziggy.

Tommy the geek pulled a handkerchief out of his

pocket and wiped his forehead with it. He gathered up his suit jacket and hat.

"Look," he said, "if the truth be known, Mr. Wrigley started the AAGPBL last year because he thought the war would mean the collapse of major-league baseball. Now we're winning the war. It won't be long until the DiMaggios and Williamses and Fellers and Greenbergs and all the rest will be coming home. When that happens, Mr. Wrigley just might shut down your whole league. I didn't want to tell you this, but that is a fact."

"He can't do that!" Ziggy exclaimed.

"Sure he can," Tommy said. "He owns the league. He shelled out two hundred thousand dollars of his own money for it already. He pays your salaries. And need I remind you that the average American worker earns ten or twenty dollars a week? The rookies among you get paid fifty dollars a week, and some of you are getting a lot more."

"This stinks," somebody in the back mumbled.

"If you don't like the way Mr. Wrigley is running things, you are free to leave and go join some other professional baseball league for girls. Good evening!"

With that, Tommy put on his hat and left. Something told me there were no other professional baseball leagues for girls.

12

First Date

THERE WAS A SOMBER MOOD IN THE LOCKER ROOM AFTER Tommy the geek left. Some of the players were angry about what he'd said, Others felt that getting paid for playing baseball was the chance of a lifetime, and they didn't mind putting on lipstick and putting up with a few silly rules to keep playing.

It was 9:30, according to the clock on the wall. Time for me to go. My cousin was home all by herself, and my father was in the hospital. I had to get back to Louisville, back to my own time.

Even though I'd had to put on a skirt, I'd had a good time. I'd stolen three bases to win the game. I'd seen a bunch of girls naked. And who was I kidding? Nothing was going to happen between me and Merle. I was just a kid. She was a grown woman.

"I'd better be going," I said as I wiped the lipstick off my mouth with my sleeve.

"Don't go!" Merle, Connie, and Mickey begged.

"You're our good luck charm," Ziggy reminded me. "Stick around."

"Whatsamatter?" Tiby asked. "Got to go home to mommy?"

"Is it past your bedtime?" Teeny smirked.

"No," I said defensively. "I have to baby-sit for my little cousin."

"How old is your cousin?" Connie asked.

"She's nine."

"Nine!" exclaimed Mickey. "When I was nine, my parents put me to work on the farm."

"Your cousin probably put herself to bed by now," Ziggy said. "What's the rush?"

Merle sidled over to me and put an arm around my shoulder. Her curly blond hair brushed against my face.

"Won't you please stay, sweetie pie?" she said, batting her eyelashes at me. "Come on, don't be a fuddy-duddy. At least let me take you out for dinner to show our appreciation for helping us win the game. I've got my own car. Pleeeease?"

"Stop corrupting the boy, Merle!" Mickey said as she handed me my clothes from her locker.

Merle was asking me out to dinner! The Blond Bombshell wanted to be alone with me! She had a car! This would be my first official date with a girl!

"Okay, I'll stay," I agreed. My cousin could wait.

"Great!" Merle said, giving me a hug. "I've got to shower and change clothes. I'll meet you at the front gate in fifteen minutes."

"Where do I change my clothes?"

Merle took me down the hall to a big closet where mops, sponges, and cleaning supplies were stored.

"I'll see you in fifteen minutes," she said, giving my hand a squeeze.

She gave my hand a squeeze! *All my life has been leading up to this night,* I said to myself as I slipped the dress down my legs. I had waited and waited and waited for puberty to arrive. First, my voice had changed. Then, hair started growing under my arms and my sweat started to stink. And now, I had a real date with a girl! An older woman, no less! Merle was probably twenty!

With all respect to Lou Gehrig, today I was the luckiest man on the face of the earth.

I washed my armpits in the sink in the storage room and dried myself off with paper towels. I put on my clothes and did my best to smooth them out. I wanted to make myself look as good as I could. There was no mirror, so I checked my reflection in a large glass jug. I wished I had a comb. Some toothpaste. Deodorant. Nicer pants.

Oh, forget about it. If Merle didn't like the way I looked, she wouldn't have asked me out on a date. Whistling to myself, I made my way to the front gate of Borchert Field.

Nobody was there when I found it, but a few minutes later I heard the sound of a car horn and

Merle shouting "Yoo-hoo! Stoshie!"

My heart shifted from fourth gear to fifth. My date had arrived. I turned around to see Merle behind the wheel of another one of those PT Cruiser clones.

And Connie Wisniewski next to her. And Tiby in the backseat with Ziggy. My heart downshifted into reverse.

"Hop in, honey pie!" Merle hollered. "Let's hit the road. We're starved!"

Nobody had told me it was going to be a group! I tried not to let my disappointment show as I climbed in the backseat between Tiby and Ziggy. *Maybe this would be even better,* I tried to convince myself. I was being taken out on a date with four girls.

They looked a lot different than they did in their baseball uniforms. Checkered blouses, jeans, and cowboy boots seemed to be the style of the Chicks.

"I thought jeans were against the rules of conduct," I said.

"The heck with the rules of conduct," Ziggy declared. "Nobody tells me what to wear."

Merle drove a few miles until we reached an area where there were more farms than houses or stores. The girls broke into the "Boogie Woogie Bugle Boy," a song I knew because my mom forced me to listen to one of her CDs, which I had titled *Stupid Old Songs to Puke By*.

I thought they would be taking me to a health

food restaurant—seeing as how they were athletes and all. But when Merle pulled into the parking lot of Johnny's Bar-B-Cue, I realized I was wrong. For all I knew, health food didn't exist in 1944.

The place was a bit of a dive, with peanut shells on the floor and cowboy stuff on the walls—ropes, saddles, hats, and so on. There was a pool table by the bar, which I assumed was the "Cue" in Johnny's Bar-B-Cue. The place was almost empty.

The girls ordered ribs, hot dogs, malteds, and Cokes. Tiby got tomato soup too. I ordered a burger.

"Something to drink?" the waitress asked.

"I'll have a Sprite," I said.

"A what?" The waitress looked up from her pad.

"Uh, Mountain Dew, please."

"I beg your pardon?"

I looked around. Everybody was looking at me funny.

"A Coke," I finally decided. "Give me a Coke."

"Sure thing."

While we waited for our food, there was a loud noise on the front steps and—to my astonishment— a chestnut horse walked right into the restaurant! And riding the horse—with a cowboy hat on her head—was Mickey Maguire.

"Yee-haw!" she bellowed.

I was sure that "yee-haw" was just one of those things you only heard in the movies and not in real life. You know, like "yippee-I-oh-ki-yay" and all that hokey cowboy talk.

Nobody seemed to think it was weird to see a woman ride into the restaurant on a horse. I assumed Mickey must do it all the time.

Mickey tied up the horse to a pole outside and joined our table. The waitress came with the food and I dug in. The burger tasted good. I realized that I hadn't eaten since the macaroni and cheese I'd shared with my cousin Samantha about four hours earlier.

"You like tomato soup?" I asked Tiby.

"No, I hate it," she said, slurping up a spoonful.

"Then why are you eating it?"

"The last time I ate it, I went four for five."

"You think the tomato soup helped you go four for five?"

"Didn't hurt," she replied.

The girls rehashed the game, congratulating me again on my baserunning and mascoting skills. But they agreed that they should have won the game much earlier than the ninth inning. If they had made a couple of key hits, if they hadn't made a few errors, they would have beaten the Peaches easily.

I thought about standing up and proposing a toast. That's what grown-ups did when they got together for meals, wasn't it? I would thank them all for being so nice to me, and I'd make a special toast to Mickey because her husband would be coming home from the war soon.

Something stopped me, though. Nobody else had mentioned it, and Mickey had acted kind of weird when she had heard the news that the Allies captured Rome. I decided to drop the idea of a toast.

When everybody was done eating and they had divied up the check, Merle leaned over to me.

"How would you like to go to a special place?" she whispered in my ear. "Just you and me?"

"Just you and m-me?" I wanted to make sure I understood her this time.

"Alone," she whispered, her blond hair brushing me again.

I gulped. This was it. She wasn't kidding this time.

"Sure," I croaked.

Merle got up from the table. "Girls," she announced, "Stoshie and I are stepping out. I'll see you in the morning."

"Have fun, you two," Mickey said. The others giggled.

Then Merle shot them a wink. I'm positive about that. It was a wink.

"Oh, we will," Merle replied, taking my hand. My heart shifted back into fifth gear as she led me to her car.

13

Alone at Last

IT HAD TO BE PAST TEN O'CLOCK NOW. THE ONLY LIGHT outside was the blinking Johnny's Bar-B-Cue sign and a thin sliver of the moon. We managed to find Merle's car in the darkness.

"You sit up front with me," Merle said. The front seat went all the way across, with no gap between the driver and the passenger. I slid in and she said, "Closer."

She gunned the engine and pulled out of the parking lot. I had no idea where she was taking me. It didn't matter, really. I was finally alone with Merle. I was out on a real date with a pretty girl! I couldn't wait to tell my friends back home.

Merle hadn't driven even a mile when she pulled off the road and into a gravel driveway with a stone pillar on either side. A few short lefts and rights past there, the headlights reflected off some slabs sticking out of the ground, and I realized we were in a cemetery.

Now, I'm not one of those kids who gets creeped out by death and stuff. People die. It's part of life. It's no big deal. I don't believe in ghosts or anything.

"This is my special place," Merle said, slowing the car to a stop. "Isn't it beautiful?"

"Peaceful," I replied. I couldn't see anything except the headstones. The only sounds were the wind blowing through the trees and the hum of the motor. "Rest in peace."

Merle switched off the headlights, and we were in near total darkness.

I had seen a lot of movies. *One of two things is going to happen right now,* I thought to myself. *She is either going to kiss me, which would be really cool. Or she is going to kill me, which wouldn't be quite so cool.* Merle didn't seem like the psychotic murderer type, so I licked my lips in preparation for my first real kiss. My heart was beating madly. I turned to face her.

"Let's take a walk," she said, flipping on the lights again.

"Uh, okay."

"I'll park the car," Merle said. "I'll meet you over there, under that tree."

If it had been anybody else, I wouldn't have gotten out of the car. I'm not stupid. It's a grave-yard. It's dark out. I'm by myself. I'm far from home, I have no money, and I'm even in the wrong decade.

But she was beautiful, so none of that mattered. I opened the door and got out of the car.

No sooner had I taken a step when she hit the gas. The tires spun, shooting gravel all over until the rubber got a grip and the car peeled away.

"Wait!" I shouted, shielding my face from the chunks of flying gravel. "Come back!"

"Ha-ha-ha-ha!" she cackled as the car turned the corner and zoomed away.

I screamed out every curse word I could think of and sprinted after her. But it was so dark that I couldn't see anything, and the sound of the motor was fading in the distance. Fearing that I might run into a tree or trip over something in the dark, I stopped.

She had done it to me again! How stupid could I be? I filed it in my mental-mistakes-to-never-make-again folder—do not get out of a car in a graveyard at night, no matter how pretty the driver is.

There was no point in running. I didn't know the way back to the restaurant. I hadn't paid attention to those lefts and rights she made, so I didn't even remember how to find the entrance to the cemetery.

"This is the thanks I get for helping the Chicks win the game," I muttered to myself bitterly. I never should have let them put that uniform on me. I never should have stolen those bases. I should have done a striptease down to my underwear right in the middle of the field. That would have shown them.

That's when I heard a sound in the woods. A movement, like a footstep. It could have just been an animal, but that was no comfort to me. What if the animal was a bear or something?

I was going to die.

If I had been smart, I would have just gone back home the minute I realized I wasn't going to meet Mickey Mantle. I could have gone home right after the game, too. None of this ever would have happened.

Wait a minute! If I could have gone home right after I arrived, and I could have gone home after the game was over, nothing was preventing me from going home right now! I had my baseball cards in my pocket. I was certainly in a nice, quiet place. I'd just bail out of here right away.

That will show Merle, I thought. *Sooner or later, she'll get worried about me and come back. But she won't find me, because I'll be home safely in the twenty-first century.* For the rest of her life, she'd think about me every time she heard that somebody was murdered. She'd wonder if it was me. She'd feel responsible. She'd feel guilty for pulling that trick on me in the graveyard. That would show her! Nobody was going to humiliate me and get away with it.

Then there was that sound again. I turned around. My eyes were beginning to adjust to the dark, but I couldn't see anybody. Maybe I was just being paranoid.

Better safe than sorry, I decided. Holding my hands in front of me, I felt my way to the nearest tombstone and sat on the ground. I took the baseball cards out of my pocket and slipped one out. I put the other cards back, and then I tried to relax. It had all been a big mistake. Soon I'd be home in my house, in my time. I'd be able to laugh about the whole thing.

In about thirty seconds, the first tingles started to hit me. I smiled. I was going home. The tingling sensation spread through my fingertips, across my arms, and down my chest. So long, 1944!

That's when a hand reached around the tombstone and grabbed me.

14

Hooray for War

"AHHHHHHHHHHHH!" I SCREAMED, DROPPING THE CARD.

I jumped up to run away, but I bumped into something or somebody. I wasn't sure which, but I knew that it wasn't there a minute ago. I turned around and bumped into something else. Suddenly there were people all around me, surrounding me, their arms clasped so I couldn't escape.

"Ahhhhhhhhhhhh!"

A flashlight beam appeared, shining up at one of their faces.

It was Mickey Maguire.

"Boo," she said simply. "Did we scare you?"

Connie, Tiby, and Ziggy turned on flashlights too as they broke out into giggles.

"Of course you scared me!" I shouted, no longer feeling any obligation to be nice to them. Now I knew why the last Chicken quit. "How could you do that to a kid? I could have had a heart attack!"

"Shhhh," Tiby said. "You'll wake the dead!" Then she cracked up.

"Don't get all hot under the collar," said Ziggy.

"How did you get out here?" I demanded, looking around for the car. "Where's Merle?"

"We walked over from Joe's," Mickey explained. "Relax. We do this to all the rookies. It's sort of our little initiation ceremony. Merle went to get some Cokes."

"I thought she . . ." My heart was still beating a million times a minute. "I thought she liked me, calling me 'sweetie' and 'honey pie' and stuff."

"She does like you," Connie assured me. "We all like you. But Merle calls everybody 'sweetie' and 'honey pie.' That's just her way."

I hung my head. I was so stupid.

"Stosh," Mickey said, "Merle is married."

"Married?"

"To an army boy."

Well, that cinched it. I would have to wait a little longer for my first date, my first kiss. Part of me was angry. Part of me, I must confess, was a little relieved. I wasn't sure if I was ready for that stuff.

The car rumbled out of the darkness. Merle cut the engine, leaving the headlights on to illuminate the area around us. There were about a dozen headstones reflecting in the dark, like a mouth full of crooked teeth. Mickey, Tiby, Connie, and Ziggy turned their flashlights off.

"I'm sorry I gave you the runaround," Merle said as she got out of the car holding a grocery bag. "No hard feelings?"

"I guess not," I said, accepting a Coke in a glass bottle.

"Come on, take a load off," Ziggy said.

The girls flopped on the grass like it was their living room, leaning back against the tombstones. Mickey opened the Cokes with an old-fashioned opener and passed the bottles around. Some of the girls lit up cigarettes. I took a big swig from my Coke. It had been a long day. Merle pulled a newspaper out of the grocery bag.

"Hey," she said, after turning to the sports section, "the Dodgers traded Eddie Stanky to the Cubs."

"How are my Indians doing?" Mickey asked.

"Terrible," Merle replied. "The Cardinals and Browns are still in first place. Musial is hitting .348."

"One day," Connie announced, "I'm gonna marry Stan Musial."

The others busted up laughing at that.

"Who would've thought St. Louis would ever top both leagues?" Tiby marveled.

"Hey," Merle said, "it says here that the Cincinnati Reds are starting this kid named Joe Nuxhall the day after tomorrow."

"So what?" Ziggy asked.

"This kid is really a kid," Merle said. "He's

fifteen years old!"

"Get out!"

"That's not much older than me," I said.

"Shows how desperate they are for players," Mickey pointed out. "They have to sign up kids. That ticks me off."

"You think they'll ever let a girl in the big leagues?" Connie asked.

"Fat chance," Ziggy said. "The only reason we even have a league is because so many guys are fighting the war."

"To war," Tiby said, taking a swig from her bottle.

"If the D day invasion succeeds," Connie predicted, "the Nazis will surrender in a year. You can bet on that. Wrigley will shut our league down. When Johnny comes marching home, so will we."

"Back to the kitchen," Ziggy said, tossing her empty bottle into the bag and cracking open another one.

"You're lucky, Mick," Merle said. "Your husband's probably on his way home right now."

"Yeah," Mickey agreed. "Lucky me."

Mickey turned her head, but a tear going down her cheek glistened in the glow of the headlights. She was trying to hide it, but I could tell that she was crying.

"What's wrong, Mick?" Connie went over and put her arms around Mickey. The others gathered around her, too.

"I don't know if I want Tom to come home,"

Mickey whimpered. "Isn't that terrible?"

"It's okay to cry, Mickey," Merle said, pulling out a handkerchief for her.

"In the last letter I got from Tom, he said he wanted me to quit playing ball when he got back," Mickey said, the words pouring out of her along with the tears. "But I don't want to quit. There's two things that I love—riding horses and playing ball."

"Do you love Tom, Mick?" Connie asked.

"I don't know," she said, wiping her face. "I honestly don't know. Tom and I hardly know each other. He went away to fight right after we got married. That was two years ago. I barely remember what he looks like without a picture."

They were all quiet as Mickey fought to control herself. She wasn't the crying type, I could tell. She didn't want to burden anyone with her personal problems.

Bugs buzzed around the headlights. The girls sipped their Cokes. A minute must have gone by before Tiby broke the silence.

"Men," she said.

That was the whole sentence, the entire thought. The others nodded in agreement and clinked their bottles together.

I knew what she meant. Every time my father did something mean or stupid, my mother used to say the same thing: "Men."

It was shorthand for "Men—can't live with them, can't live without them." It seemed to sum up everything. And whenever my mother did something my father didn't like, he would shake his head and say one word: "Women."

"We're not all bad," I said, feeling a certain duty to defend my gender. "Some of us are actually good guys."

They all turned to look at me, as if they had forgotten that one of the enemy was in their midst.

"I miss my dad," Ziggy said. "I've never been away from home so long."

"Me neither," the others agreed.

"My brother taught me how to play ball," Connie said. "He gave me my first baseball glove."

"You had a glove?" Merle marveled. "Honey, my family was so poor during the Depression that we played ball wearing work gloves. Our bat was the end of a rake, and we used cow pies for bases."

Tiby burst out laughing, and even Mickey smiled a little.

"Wait a minute," Tiby said, "you slid into cow pies?"

"Sure 'nuff!"

"If I was sliding into a cow pie," Tiby said, "I'd want to be wearing work gloves too!"

"Well, we wouldn't slide in headfirst!" Merle exclaimed. "That would be disgusting!"

All of us broke out in guffaws.

"I don't know about you girls," Mickey said, "but when I was growing up, I would do anything to play ball."

"Ain't that the truth," Ziggy agreed.

"I'd even play football with the boys," Tiby said. "The girls used to laugh at me. They thought I was really weird."

"You are really weird," Merle remarked, which sent the rest of us into fits of giggles.

While they swapped more stories of growing up during the Depression, I lay back on the grass and put my arms behind my head to get more comfortable. It had never even crossed my mind that anyone would think I was weird or that it was wrong for me to play a sport. But then, up until today, I thought girls had no place on a baseball diamond. A lot had changed since 1944, but a lot of things were still the same.

There must have been a million stars in the sky. I tried to pick out the constellations, but in just a few minutes I was fast asleep.

15

News

"STOSH! WAKE UP! WAKE UP!"

I felt like I had been asleep for a hundred years. I must have been dreaming of a fire or something. It felt so real, the smell of burning was still in my nose.

"Huh?" I muttered. "Mom? Where am I?"

I opened my eyes to see Mickey Maguire's face over me. She was in uniform. I was lying on the floor of the Chicks locker room.

"You fell asleep last night at the cemetery," she whispered, as if she didn't want anyone to know we had been out so late. "We tried to wake you, but you were out like a light. It started raining and we didn't know where to take you, so we brought you here."

"What time is it?" I asked, sitting up. The Chicks were at their lockers, already in uniform.

"Eight o'clock in the morning," Mickey said. "We have a game at ten. Stosh, your parents must be worried sick! Give me your phone number. I'll call them and explain everything."

"You can't call them."

"Why not?" Mickey asked. "Don't you have a phone?"

I couldn't tell her that it was impossible to call my parents because my parents weren't even born yet. If I told her I'd traveled back in time to 1944 with a baseball card, she would never believe me.

"No, we don't have a phone," I lied.

"Well, where do you live?" Mickey asked. "Merle can drive you home."

"I live in Louisville."

"Kentucky? How in the world did you get to Milwaukee? That's almost four hundred miles! Did you run away from home?"

"No, it's nothing like that." I don't like to lie, but every so often you have to. "I took the train. I'll head back this morning. My mom knows all about it."

That seemed to satisfy Mickey, who began taping up her legs. Now fully awake, I was able to think more clearly and figure out my situation. I had left home around six o'clock the night before. It was eight o'clock in the morning now. My cousin had probably stayed up late watching TV and would sleep late in the morning. My mother had probably stayed over at the hospital and wouldn't be home for a few hours. With a little luck, I wouldn't get into trouble for being away all night.

The Chicks locker room looked like an emergency room. Mickey was taping her legs. Connie Wisniewski was adjusting her knee brace. The others were applying ointments and medicines to their bruises and strawberries. A couple of new girls had already been brought in to replace the sick and wounded.

"My blister is killing me," Ziggy complained as she hobbled around.

"I can take care of that for you," Connie said.

"Oh yeah? How?"

Ziggy hopped up on the training table, and Connie examined the foot. There was a blister about the size of a quarter on Ziggy's heel.

"This is a piece of cake," Connie said as she went to a cabinet mounted on the wall. She came back with some tissues and a single-edged razor blade in her hand.

"You're going to slice it off?" Ziggy squeaked.

"Of course! You can't play ball with one of those on your foot. Just hold still."

Ziggy leaned back so she wouldn't have to watch and gripped the sides of the table with both hands. Expertly, Connie sliced off the blister, to the disgust of the others, who couldn't resist the temptation to gather around and view the operation.

"See?" Connie said. "All done. Good as new. The show is over, girls."

The players returned to what they had been

doing, and Ziggy held a tissue to her foot. There was a soft knock on the door to the dugout and somebody opened it. Max Carey came in with his ever-present clipboard.

"Gather around, everyone," he said, and the players instantly obeyed. "Time for a little lesson in fundamentals."

A few groans were heard as Carey wheeled in a large blackboard from behind the lockers. With a piece of chalk, he drew this picture.

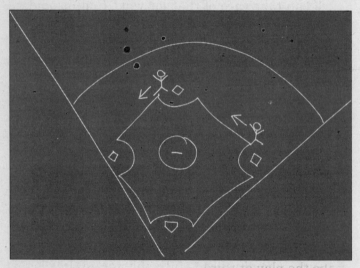

**With a piece of chalk, Carey drew this picture.
"We're in the field. Bottom of the ninth."**

"Here's the situation. We're in the field. Bottom of the ninth. We have a one-run lead. Runners at first and second. One out. The count is two balls and one strike. Now I want each of you to tell me what you are thinking at this moment. Pitcher first. Connie?"

"I'm thinking, don't make the pitch too good," Connie said immediately. "I have two balls to work with. But I don't want to walk her because that would put the tying run in scoring position. They might put on the hit-and-run play. Keep an eye on the runner at second. I want a double play, but I'll take an out. On a grounder to me, I'll throw to third to get the lead runner and maybe start a double play. If she bunts toward third, I'll try and make the play there. If she bunts toward first, I'll throw to first. If the batter gets a hit, I'll back up home plate."

"Very good," Carey said. "Mickey, you're next."

"I'm thinking, how well does this batter hit Connie?" Mickey said. "Is she a pull hitter, or does she hit to the opposite field? Is she hot or cold? Is she a low-ball hitter? What's her weakness? How did we get her out last time? Who's on deck? Should I call for a pitchout? Is Connie getting tired? Should I call for a fastball, curve, or change up? Watch for the double steal. Be ready to pounce on a bunt, maybe try to make the play at third."

I just sat there, my mouth open. I'm a pretty decent ballplayer, but I never saw the game at this level. There was so much to think about, so many possible things that could happen in any situation. It was like a game of chess.

"Left field next." Max Carey pointed. "Tiby?"

"I'm wondering, should I play this hitter straightaway or shade her to the left or right? If the batter singles, I have a good shot at throwing the runner out at the plate. If there's an extra-base hit—"

A knock at the door to the dugout stopped her.

"Who is it?" Carey barked.

A woman came in. She was older and all dolled up in a fancy blue dress, frilly hat, and high-heeled shoes.

"I beg your pardon," the lady said, pronouncing every word slowly, clearly, and politely. "My name is Judith Vanderbilt, and I represent the Helena Rubinstein School of Charm."

"Get out," Carey said gruffly. "We're not interested in your products. We have a game soon, for crying out loud."

"You don't understand," the woman said. "Mr. Philip Wrigley commissioned our services. He is the owner of the league, if I am not mistaken. Mr. Wrigley most specifically insisted I speak to the players at this time."

Carey took off his cap and slapped it against his knee. "Make it snappy," he said, sitting down on a stool.

"When you become a player in the All-American Girls Baseball League, you have reached the highest position that a girl can attain in this sport," the charm school lady began. "You have certain responsibilities because you are in the limelight. Your actions and appearance both on and off the field reflect on the whole profession. It is your duty to do your best to uphold the standard of this profession."

Max Carey rolled his eyes.

"It is most desirable that each girl be at all times presentable and attractive," the charm school lady continued. "Study your own beauty culture possibilities, and without overdoing your beauty treatment at the risk of attaining gaudiness, practice the little measure that will reflect well on your appearance and personality as a real all-American girl."

Max Carey shook his head and looked at his watch.

"Because of your strenuous activity on the diamond, you are exposed to dirt, grime, dust, and perspiration," the charm school lady said. "When you bathe, use cleansing cream around your neck as well as over your face. Apply a lotion to keep your hands as lovely as possible."

A few of the girls snickered. Max Carey closed his eyes and rubbed the bridge of his nose with his fingertips.

"Always secure your stockings so they are smooth and neat and remain in place. Arrange your hair neatly in a manner that will best retain its natural style despite vigorous play. Deodorant keeps you fresh and gives you assurance and confidence in your social contacts. You should walk with poise at all times."

Merle raised her hand, and the charm school lady called on her.

"What's a poy?"

"Poise," Mrs. Vanderbilt repeated. "It means dignity and confidence. Walk with poise. Are there any other questions?"

"Yeah," Ziggy said. "How is any of this gonna help me make the double play?"

The players laughed and Max Carey got up off his stool.

"Okay," he said, "can we get back to our meeting now? We got a game to play in less than an hour."

"There are still a few more things I would like to go over about grooming and etiquette—"

The phone on the wall rang behind me. Max Carey gestured for me to pick it up.

"Milwaukee Chicks locker room," I answered.

"May I speak with Dorothy Maguire, please," a serious-sounding woman said.

"Sure, who's this?"

"Her mother, in Cleveland."

"Mickey, it's for you," I said, and handed her the phone.

Mickey listened for a few seconds, then closed her eyes and leaned heavily against the wall. The phone dropped from her hand.

"Get out!" Max Carey ordered the charm school lady.

"But I still have a lot—"

"Get out!"

The charm school lady looked shocked and insulted, scooting out the door without saying another word. Tears were running down Mickey's face and she was sobbing quietly.

"Tom's dead," she said simply. Then her knees buckled and she slid down against the wall until she was sitting on the floor. The rest of the team rushed to her side. Max Carey hung his head.

I picked up the phone. Mickey's mother was still on the line. She told me that Corporal Tom Maguire had been killed in action several days before while fighting in Italy. His body had not yet been recovered. She didn't have any other information. I told her how sorry everyone was and hung up the phone.

For a few minutes, nobody said anything. Mickey's teammates just held her as she cried. Those of us who had been with her the night before knew she wasn't all that happy in her marriage. I remembered that she had said her husband was going to make her quit playing ball as soon as he came home. If he was dead, she wouldn't have to quit. I know it was wrong to think that her husband's death could be a good thing, but I thought it all the same. I wondered if she was thinking that, too.

Mickey must have loved her husband to a certain extent. It was several minutes and a bunch of tissues later when she was able to get to her feet.

"Mickey," Max Carey said as he came over and put an arm around her, "sit this one out today. Take as much time as you need to come back."

"I can catch, Mr. Carey," I volunteered.

"No," Mickey said. "I want to play."

"Go home," Max pleaded. "Rest up. We'll talk tomorrow."

"A split lip didn't keep me out of the lineup," Mickey said, strapping on a shin guard. "A busted toe didn't keep me out of the lineup. This won't keep me out of the lineup either."

Carey sighed and patted her on the back.

"I'll have them make an annoucement over the PA for the press and the fans," he said.

"No announcement!" Mickey asserted in a voice that said she meant it. She strapped on her other shin guard and led the Chicks out to the dugout.

16

Heading Home

THE TIME HAD COME FOR ME TO GO. THERE WAS NOTHING more for me to do in 1944. I was alone in the locker room now. It was quiet. I still had my baseball cards.

"Ladies and gentlemen," I heard the public address announcer boom, "in ten minutes, the Milwaukee Chicken will throw a strike for freedom!"

I stopped. The chicken suit was in the open locker next to Mickey's.

There was no reason for me to stay. I didn't have to participate in any silly promotion. It wouldn't make any difference whether or not I could throw a stupid ball through a stupid hole in Hitler's face.

But I wanted to. I wanted another chance. I wanted to redeem myself for yesterday.

I put on the stupid chicken suit.

When I opened the door leading to the dugout, I saw one of the strangest sights I had ever witnessed. The field was on fire.

The infield dirt from first base to third was ablaze, with some of the flames reaching two or three feet high. Black smoke rose up from the diamond.

I was about to run for help or get a fire extinguisher, but the Chicks, milling around the dugout, seemed totally unconcerned.

"What's going on?" I asked.

"It rained last night," Connie Wisniewski told me, "so they spread gasoline on the field and lit it to dry it off."

That seemed like the silliest idea in the world to me. Hadn't these people ever heard of a tarp? But the gasoline must have worked. Soon the flames died down, and those two burly guys named Bob went out to smooth the dirt with rakes. The players went out on the field to toss balls around.

Smoke was still hanging over the diamond when I spotted somebody in the distance hop over the center field fence and onto the field. It was an African-American, I noticed first. As the figure got closer, I could tell it was a girl. She couldn't have been more than eighteen or so. Under her arm was a baseball glove.

As the girl marched toward second base, one by one the Chicks noticed her. They stopped playing catch with each other. The girl didn't turn to look at them. She was heading for the dugout.

Max Carey had been writing on his clipboard, but he looked up when he noticed the sound of balls popping into gloves had stopped. The African-American girl walked right up to him.

"Are you Mr. Carey?" she asked.

"I am. What can I do for you?"

"I heard that your first baseman broke her leg yesterday," the girl said.

"That's right," Carey replied.

"My name is Toni Stone, and I can play first base."

Carey looked the girl up and down silently, the way he would size up a prospect. The Chicks were all staring at her, too. Toni Stone put her hands on her hips.

I noticed for the first time that all the Chicks were white. All the Rockford Peaches had been white, too. It was an all-white league, I realized. African-Americans were still banned from baseball. Jackie Robinson wouldn't break the color barrier with the Brooklyn Dodgers until 1947—three years in the future.

"I can run a hundred yards in eleven seconds," Toni Stone told Carey. "I can hit. I can throw. I can field. I'd like a tryout, Mr. Carey."

He looked at Toni Stone for a long time. I thought he just might give the girl a chance. The Chicks, after all, had been shorthanded even before Dolores Klosowski broke her leg.

"I'm sorry, Miss Stone," Carey finally said. "The league holds tryouts in the spring before the season starts. I can't sign anyone now."

Toni Stone looked in Carey's eyes, like she was trying to figure out if he was telling the truth or not. So was I. Carey went back to his clipboard.

"I heard some other girls were signed up in midseason," Stone persisted. "White girls."

"I'm sorry," Carey said. "It is not my decision."

Toni Stone pawed the dirt with her foot for a moment.

"Didn't want to play ball in a dress anyway," she said, before turning around and jogging back toward center field. The Chicks resumed their warm-ups.

Soon the smoke was gone and fans had filled most of the bleachers. The two Bobs carried out the giant Hitler head and set it up at home plate. I stretched my legs and windmilled my arm around to get ready to throw my strike for freedom.

"Ladies and gentlemen," said the public address announcer, "please direct your attention to the home plate area. If the Milwaukee Chicken can throw a ball through Hitler's tooth, each and every person in the ballpark this morning will receive a free pass to see *Meet Me in St. Louis* starring Judy Garland, now showing in air-conditioned comfort at the Palace Theater on Wisconsin Avenue."

"Boooooo!" rained down on me as I jogged toward the mound. A few people threw things on the field.

"That chicken can't hit the broad side of a barn!" somebody hollered.

"You'd better do better than last night!" yelled somebody else.

One of the Bobs handed me the ball. The Chicks stopped warming up and began to clap for me. The fans picked up the rhythm and joined in.

"You can do it, sweetie pie!" Merle hollered through cupped hands.

I gripped the ball and put my foot on the pitching rubber. Hitler was grinning at me with a maniacal smirk. I focused on the hole in his teeth.

Bringing my arms up over my head and kicking my leg high, I wound up and let the ball fly, moving forward with so much force that the chicken head fell off.

The ball sailed right through Hitler's gap-toothed grin.

"Yayyyyyyyyyyyyyyyyyyy!"

The crowd went nuts, clapping and cheering so loudly that the birds nesting on the roof of Borchert Field flew away in a panic. I raised my chicken wings in triumph.

Connie, Mickey, Tiby, and Merle rushed to me and hoisted me up on their shoulders. They paraded me around the field while the fans continued screaming. Finally, the Chicks deposited me in the dugout. Max Carey even came over to shake my hand.

"You got good stuff there," he said as he

clapped me on the back.

"This has been great," I told them all, "but I've got to go now."

"We'll miss you, honey pie," Merle said, planting a kiss on my cheek.

"We have a present for you," Connie said. She reached under the bench and pulled out an envelope about the size of a folded newspaper. I opened it, and there was a photo inside.

On the back, they had all signed their names and written little messages, like "Stoshie, you're the best!" and "To Stosh, an honorary Chick."

"This is"—I tried to find the right word—"swell!"

On the back, they had all signed their names and written little messages, like "Stoshie, you're the best!"

I thanked them all, and the girls ran out on the field for batting practice. Mickey pulled me aside and slipped ten one-dollar bills in my hand.

"We took up a collection," she said. "This ought to be enough to get you back to Louisville, and maybe get a couple of hot dogs, too."

She wrapped her arms around me. As she rested her head on my shoulder for a moment, I felt her tears on my neck.

"I'm sorry about your husband," I said.

"Thanks," she replied simply, and then she grabbed a bat and ran out onto the field.

I went into the locker room to change my clothes. As I was peeling off the chicken suit, one of the burly Bobs came in.

"Hey, nice throw, you lucky stiff," he said.

"Thanks. I hope you enjoy the movie."

"I will," Bob said. "By the way, Mickey Maguire told me to tell you how to get to the train station. It's just three blocks away. If you go out the left field exit and walk down that street, you can't miss it."

"Thanks."

I had no intention of going to the train station. I didn't need any train to take me home. I had a baseball card. My plan was to just sit by a locker, wait for the tingling sensation to begin, and blow out of there.

The only problem was Bob. He had hauled out a mop and a bucket and begun swabbing the floor. It didn't look like he would be done anytime soon.

I decided to find another place. The ballpark was way too noisy and crowded. I grabbed my envelope containing the team picture and left the locker room.

Maybe there's a little park or a garden nearby, I thought as I made my way through the stands, looking for the way out of Borchert Field. The left field exit was the nearest one, so I used it.

A row of apartment buildings lined the street. The sidewalks were empty. I kept walking, thinking the train station actually might be a good spot. Just as I made the decision to go there, I heard footsteps coming up behind me.

17

Enemies and a Friend

THE FOOTSTEPS I HEARD COMING UP BEHIND ME COULD have been anybody's. They could have been those of a little old lady walking to the market. Or they could have been trouble. I decided to risk a little embarrassment and turn around.

They were trouble.

"Remember me?"

I didn't, at first. It took a moment or two to recognize him. Then I remembered—the kid who had shown up the day before to be the Chicks mascot. I had taken the job in his place and told him to go away.

How did he know what I looked like? I wondered. I had had the chicken suit on when I met him. Then I remembered that the head fell off when I threw the ball at Hitler. The kid must have been watching me like a hawk. Now he was staring at me with a cold look in his eyes. Playing it cool seemed to be the way to go in this situation.

"Sure I remember you," I said cheerfully. "Hi! I'm leaving now. Taking the train home. The mascot job is open if you still want it."

I was ready to turn around and continue on my merry way, but the kid was still staring coldly at me.

"Nobody makes a monkey out of me," he said.

I've had my share of fights in my life. I know how to use my fists. But the last thing I wanted to do was get into a fight now. Oh, I could take the kid, I felt certain of that. He was no bigger than me. I really wanted to say, "What are you going to do about it?" But I didn't. All I wanted to do was go home.

"I'm sorry," I said. "They asked me if I was the new mascot and I said yes. My mistake."

That should have been the end of it. I had apologized. What more did he want from me? To get down on my knees and beg his forgiveness? That wasn't going to happen.

"I ain't here to listen to your sob story."

The kid let out a whistle, and five other guys came out from the alley behind him. A couple of them were holding baseball bats, and I didn't think they'd brought them to play a game. I was in real trouble.

"What do you want?" I asked, taking a step backward.

"You," one of them said. "We're gonna knock your block off."

"When somebody messes with one of us," another boy said, "they're messing with all of us."

This was not good. My heart and brain were suddenly racing. I couldn't fight them all. I might get myself killed. There was nothing I could say that would make them leave me alone. I could scream for help. Not very manly, but it might work. Why did this stuff always happen to me? Why did I have to pick on a kid who was a member of a gang?

"Whatsamatter, kid? Ya scared?"

There were ten singles in my pocket, I remembered. That's a week's pay for a lot of people in 1944. Maybe if I chucked the bills up in the air and made a run for it, I could get to the train station a few blocks away. I didn't need the money, and they would probably rather have ten bucks than beat me up.

Just as I was reaching into my pocket for the bills, a thumping noise came up from behind the six boys. It sounded like hoofbeats. When they all turned around, I saw a horse galloping directly toward us. It was Chico's Flame, with Mickey Maguire on top.

One of the kids let out a curse. Just as Mickey was about to mow them down, the boys scattered out of the way like bowling pins.

"Hop on, Stosh!" Mickey hollered.

I climbed up behind her and grabbed her around

the waist tightly. She flicked the reins and Chico's Flame took off. I turned around to see the boys waving their fists and bats at me.

"How did you know—"

"Max noticed a boy following you through the stands," Mickey explained. "He was going to send the two Bobs to chase the kid away, but I told him I could get here quicker."

Mickey steered Chico's Flame up the street and right into a big building that said NORTH WESTERN RAILROAD DEPOT on it. A few people recognized Mickey and shouted greetings to her. I hopped off, gave Chico's Flame a pat, and thanked Mickey. She wished me well and galloped right back out the door.

It wasn't very likely that those boys would have followed us to the train station, but I didn't want to take the chance. I ran to the ticket window.

"Where you heading, sonny?" the ticket seller asked. "And what's your rush?"

"Anywhere," I replied, gasping for breath. "When is the next train?"

"The 9:55 to St. Louis, with a stop in Chicago, is just arriving on track three. I think you can still make it."

"Sounds good."

The fare was $4.50. I fished five singles out of my pocket and slid them under the bars. He gave me the change and a ticket.

"There he is!" somebody shouted as soon as I left

the ticket window.

I turned around to see those six jerks at the door Mickey Maguire had just left. She couldn't help me now. I was on my own. They were coming my way.

"All aboard for Chicago and St. Louis! Track three. All aboard!"

Clutching my envelope, I made a dash for track three and got there just as the train started moving. I jumped on the last car as the train was pulling away from the station.

Peering out the side, I saw the boys on the platform. They couldn't catch me now. I let out a sigh of relief.

I wasn't sure whether or not they'd understand, but just for the fun of it I gave them the finger.

The train had one of those big old steam engines, with a fancy dining car and uniformed conductors walking up and down, punching people's tickets. I had hoped to find a quiet car where I could pull out my baseball cards and send myself home, but this train was jammed with passengers.

"Next stop Chicago!" a conductor hollered.

After walking through two cars, I finally found an empty seat next to a husky kid with a crew cut. He looked about my age. He was wearing a baseball uniform that said BAXTER SPRINGS WHIZ KIDS on it.

"You play ball?" I said as I sat down next to him, realizing instantly what a stupid question that was. Of course the kid played ball.

"Yup," he replied.

That was all he said. When fifteen minutes had gone by and he didn't say a word, I figured the kid was just the quiet type and I should leave him alone.

"You?" he suddenly asked, startling me.

"Huh?"

"Do you play ball?"

"Oh yeah," I told him. "Little League mostly. Pickup games too, if anybody's around. I live for baseball. Always did."

"Me too," he replied. "When I was little, we had this old tin barn next to our house. My dad would pitch tennis balls to me against the barn. We did it for hours. It would get dark and my mom would be hollerin' for us to come in for dinner. Dad would say, 'Your belly can wait. Ten more pitches.' My dad taught me everything I know about the game."

"Same with me," I told him.

He said he was on his way back home to Oklahoma. The kid spoke with a soft drawl, and he had an easy laugh. I liked him right away. We had a lot in common, too. We were both about the same age, we both loved baseball, and we both dreamed of playing in the big leagues one day.

We were both poor, too, but his family was even poorer than mine. He told me his dad was a miner and part-time sharecropper. They lived in a two-bedroom house, with two parents and five kids. He didn't have a toilet in his house. One year, he said, it rained for days and days. His family lost everything they had in the flood.

"Next stop Chicago!" yelled the conductor as he came down the aisle, collecting tickets. "Change for Peoria, Kansas City, Wichita, and Tulsa."

The kid seemed to enjoy telling stories, and I enjoyed listening to him. But as the train was slowing down to stop in Chicago, he grabbed the bag under his seat and said he had to switch to the train for Tulsa, which was near his home.

"I hope to see you again when we're in the majors someday," he said as he got up from the seat.

"Yeah, me too."

"Hey," he said, patting his pockets, "you and me oughta swap signatures. That way, if one of us makes the bigs, the other will have his autograph."

"Okay."

The train squeaked to a stop, and just about everybody got off. The kid found a piece of paper and a pen. He ripped the paper in half and handed me one of the pieces, along with the pen. I wrote my name and gave him back the paper and pen. He wrote his name on the other piece of paper, folded it once, and handed it to me.

"Bye," he said, hustling down the aisle. "Good luck."

"Bye."

He got off just before the train started to pull away from the station. Through my window, I saw the kid on the platform. I unfolded the piece of paper he had given me.

Mickey Mantle

For almost an hour, I had been sitting next to thirteen-year-old Mickey Mantle, and I hadn't even known it!

I bolted up from my seat. For almost an hour, I had been sitting next to thirteen-year-old Mickey Mantle, and I hadn't even known it! I pounded on the window, trying to get his attention.

"Mickey!" I shouted. "Mickey!"

Finally, he turned around and looked at me. The train was starting to accelerate.

"The drain!" I screamed. "There's a hidden drain outlet in the outfield at Yankee Stadium! Don't step on it!"

"What?"

Mickey cupped a hand to his ear and looked at me with a puzzled expression on his face. He got smaller and smaller.

18

Home

I COULDN'T BELIEVE IT. I HAD ACTUALLY MET MICKEY Mantle, but he hadn't heard the one thing I had gone back in time to tell him. Things just never seem to work out the way you think they will.

The train had pretty much emptied out at Chicago. There were a couple of heads poking over the tops of seats at the front of the car, but I didn't think they would bother me. The clickety-clack of the wheels on the track was actually relaxing, in a way. It felt like a good environment to use my "special gift."

I slipped the big envelope under my arm and pulled my new baseball cards out of my pocket. Thankfully, after all I had been through, I hadn't lost them.

It didn't matter which card I used, so I didn't waste time going through them. Picking a card at random, I closed my eyes.

While waiting for the tingling to begin, I thought about everything that had happened to me from the moment I'd arrived in 1944 until the moment I was about to leave. Seeing the Chicks coming out of the shower room (that was a high point!). Meeting the great Max Carey. Dressing up as a chicken. Dressing up as a girl! Helping the Chicks win the game. The graveyard. Toni Stone. Being chased by those jerks. Sitting next to Mickey Mantle. It had been some trip.

Soon I felt the tingles in my fingertips. It was the best feeling in the world. It meant I was going home.

The vibrations rolled up my arms and down my chest. There was no turning back now.

"Next stop St. Louis," a conductor said as he came down the aisle.

It didn't matter to me now. I kept my eyes shut as the tingling sensation flowed down my legs. I was almost there.

"Next stop— Whoa! Kid, are you okay? Oh, man, this boy is fading away!"

When I opened my eyes again, I was sitting on the couch in our living room, just as I had been when I left. The envelope was still under my arm. Mickey Mantle's autograph was still in my pocket. My cousin Samantha was curled up in a ball on the floor below me, watching Bugs Bunny on TV.

"Good morning," I said, causing her to jump up with a start.

"Where were you?" she asked. "I've been looking all over the house!"

"I wasn't in the house. I was in Milwaukee in 1944. Now do you believe I can travel through time?"

"It was a trick," Samantha insisted. "You used mirrors or something."

"Maybe this will convince you," I said, pulling the team photo of the Chicks out of its envelope and handing it to her.

Samantha had a smirk on her face, but it vanished when she realized what she was looking at.

"I met your hero, Connie Wisniewski," I told her. "Flip it over."

She turned over the photo and looked at the other side. With each autograph she recognized, her eyes got wider. With each note the players had written to me, her mouth dropped open a bit more.

"It . . . works?"

"Of course it works!" I exclaimed. "You tricked me, slipping that Mickey Maguire card in place of my Mickey Mantle card!"

"I . . . I never thought you were really going to travel through time," she said. "I thought you were pulling a joke on me, so I pulled one on you first. Oh, it doesn't matter now, does it? What was it like in 1944? Were they nice? Tell me everything."

"First things first," I said. "Where's the Mickey

Mantle card you took out of my hand?"

"I sold it," she replied. "For ten dollars."

"What?" I exploded. "That card is worth seventy-five thousand dollars! How could you—"

"Just kidding," she said, pulling the plastic card holder from her pocket and handing it to me.

Girls!

"Gimme that!" I said, snatching it away from her.

"Oh, Joey, your baseball coach left a bunch of messages on the answering machine about some game you have this afternoon. You told me not to pick up the phone."

I had forgotten all about the game. I had figured that the first thing I would do when I got home was to go over to the hospital to see how my dad was doing.

I was about to call the hospital when a car pulled up outside. I looked out the window and saw that my mom was home. I took the team photo of the Chicks and hid it under the couch.

"Don't tell my mother I left you alone all night," I warned Samantha. "She'll ground me for the rest of my life if she finds out."

"I told you, I didn't need any baby-sitter, any-way," Samantha said.

"Just don't tell her!"

Mom came in and gave each of us a hug. Her eyes looked tired, like she had been up all night. Her hair needed combing or something.

"Have you two been good?" she asked, sitting

heavily on the couch. "What mischief did you get into while I was away?"

I shot Samantha a look and she shot me one back.

"Nothing much," I said casually. "We watched TV mostly. How is Dad?"

Before Mom could answer, there was a knock at the front door. I went to get it. Coach Tropiano was standing on the front porch. I let him in.

"I couldn't reach you by phone," he said, "so I thought I'd stop by. I just wanted to see if your dad was okay, Joe, and to see if you might be able to play today. It's a big game, our last game."

I turned to Mom. She motioned for me to come over to her, and took my hand in hers when I did.

"Dad is doing better now, Joey," she said. "But he . . . doesn't have any feeling."

"You mean he's paralyzed?"

She nodded her head, and I collapsed in her arms.

"Below the neck," she said softly.

"Uncle Bill is paralyzed?" Samantha asked, bursting instantly into tears.

"I'm sorry!" Coach Tropiano blurted out, backing toward the door. "I shouldn't have come over at a time like this. My deepest condolences, Mrs. Stoshack. I'll call you in a few days to see how you're doing, Joe."

"Wait," I said, getting to my feet. "Don't go, Coach."

Coach Tropiano paused in the doorway.

"What is it, Joe?" he asked. "Is there anything I can do to help?"

"Yes," I replied. "Start me."

"Joe," the coach said, "I completely understand if you don't come to the game. The guys on the team will understand, too. I'll make an announcement."

"No announcement," I said. "I want to play, Coach. Is it okay, Mom?"

My mother nodded her head. I went upstairs to put my uniform on.

ENJOY A REAL SPORTS THRILL!
MILWAUKEE vs. **ROCKFORD**
TOMORROW---6:00 P.M.---BORCHERT FIELD
ADMISSION—ADULTS, **95¢** CHILDREN, 30¢
Box Seats, $1.40   (Under 12 Years)
Thrilling Games Every Day Through July 4th!
COME TO COMFORTABLE, EASY-TO-REACH BORCHERT FIELD

Facts and Fictions

EVERYTHING YOU READ IN THIS BOOK WAS TRUE. THAT is, except for the stuff I made up. It's only fair to let you know which was which.

First, the facts . . .

Mickey, Connie, Tiby, Merle, and all the other players in the All-American Girls Professional Baseball League (AAGPBL) were real people. So was Max Carey, the Chicks' manager. During World War II, when so many men were away fighting, suddenly American women had the opportunity to enter fields in which they were not welcome before, and professional baseball was one of them. Chicago Cubs owner Philip K. Wrigley (whose father started the gum company in 1891 with $32) founded the AAGPBL in 1943, mainly to keep baseball alive during the war.

After two seasons, with the war won (almost a year after D day, Germany surrendered on May 7, 1945), Wrigley sold the league to his advertising director for $10,000. The AAGPBL thrived in the late 1940s, and closed up shop in 1954.

Why did it die? Lots of reasons. Americans had new things to do. Drive-in movies. Bowling. NASCAR started in 1948. The NBA was founded in 1949. Young women were getting married and starting a baby boom.

And, of course, there was television. In 1945, there were only seven thousand TV sets in the entire United States. Six years later, there were ten million. People could watch major-league games for free in their living rooms, so why go out for anything less? Many men's minor-league teams went out of business at this time, too.

After their poor start in 1944, the Milwaukee Chicks came back strong. They went on to finish the season at 70-45 and win the AAGPBL championship, beating the Kenosha Comets in a seven-game play-off.

Sadly, that was the only year the team existed. Due to poor attendance, they were moved to Grand Rapids, Michigan, in 1945, where they remained for ten years. Wrigley really did hire the Milwaukee Symphony to play before games, in hopes of increasing attendance. It didn't work.

Borchert Field (which was actually nowhere near the train station) was torn down in 1954. Interstate 43 now covers the site.

Connie Wisniewski was the AAGPBL player of the year in 1945. When the league switched to overhand pitching in 1948, she became an outfielder and led the league in homers one season. After her baseball career, she worked at General Motors and also opened a restaurant called The Chicks' Dugout. She died in 1995.

Alma "Ziggy" Ziegler was player of the year in 1950. She became a court reporter. Thelma "Tiby" Eisen worked at General Telephone in California, where she became one of the first female equipment installers.

Merle "the Blond Bombshell" Keagle died from cancer in her thirties. Doris Tetzlaff became a physical education teacher and died in 1998.

Chicks manager Max Carey was president of the AAGPBL from 1945 to 1949. He was elected to the Baseball Hall of Fame in 1961 and died in 1976.

A fifteen-year-old boy named Joe Nuxhall really did pitch for the Cincinnati Reds on June 10, 1944. He didn't last one inning, walking five batters and giving up two hits. But Nuxhall came back in 1952 and had a productive fifteen-year career in the majors.

The players in the AAGPBL really were required to go to charm school. Everything the charm school lady said in this book came directly from *The Charm School Guide,* which was given to all the players in the league. The rules of conduct are also real, though I shortened them.

The facts in this book came from interviewing Mickey Maguire's son Rick Chapman; her sister Jean Cobb; and her teammates Tiby Eisen, Alma Ziegler, Vivian Anderson, Viola Thompson Griffin, Helen Steffes, Helen Hannah, and Sarah Lonetto.

I also got a lot of information by reading *A Whole New Ball Game* by Sue Macy; *Girls of Summer: In Their Own League* by Lois Browne; *When Women Played Hardball* by Susan E. Johnson; *Women at Play: The Story of Women in Baseball* by Barbara Gregorich; *Women in Baseball: The Forgotten History* by Gai Ingham Berlage; and W. C. Madden's reference books about the AAGPBL.

After the AAGPBL folded, the women went on with their lives and rarely talked about the league. Mickey Maguire never even told her children that she had been a professional ballplayer! The surviving players held a fortieth anniversary celebration in 1982, and in 1988 the Baseball Hall of Fame included them in a new exhibit titled "Women and Baseball." But the world didn't really learn about the AAGPBL until 1992, when the movie *A League of Their Own* was released.

You may have found it odd that the women of the AAGPBL were called "girls" in this book. In 1944, women were often called girls and did not take offense at it. Times have changed.

Now the fictions . . .

The teams of the AAGPBL did not have mascots, and men were never allowed to play. I must admit I made that part up to get Stosh into the action.

While Chicks first baseman Dolores Klosowski did break her leg during a game in 1944, it happened a week after the events in this book, on June 14.

While Toni Stone was a real person and was eighteen years old in 1944, she never tried out for the AAGPBL. She did play second base in the Negro League in 1953, hitting a respectible .243. Two African-American women worked out with the AAGPBL in 1951, but they were not signed up.

The news that the Allies captured Rome was actually in the newspapers the same day that D day was reported, but for the sake of the story, I placed it a few days later.

Finally, Joe Stoshack and the characters from the present day do not exist. Time travel is impossible with baseball cards or any other way, darn it.

One more thing . . .

It's true that three days after D day, Mickey Maguire got the news that her husband, Tom, had been killed in action, and she insisted on playing that day. But there is more to the story. Two

Dorothy Maguire's Husband War Victim

Drama unknown to the crowd transpired in the clubhouse at Lake Front Stadium Saturday night. Just before the Milwaukee club took the field for practice, Dorothy Maguire, catcher, formerly with Racine, was notified in a long distance telephone call from her mother in Cleveland., of the death of her husband. A corporal in the army, he was killed in action in Italy; he served overseas the past two years. The last letter she had from him was four months ago.

The catcher insisted on playing the game, but out of deference to her wishes, no announcement of the casualty message was made to the public. She also caught the second game Sunday. So the show goes on for Maguire!

A human drama which was played on the diamonds of the All-American Girls league this season has come to a happy ending—almost a story-book ending. On Saturday night, June 10, Dorothy (Mickey) Maguire, who is first-string catcher for the Milwaukee Chicks and formerly a member of the Racine Belles, received word that her husband, Corp. Thomas J. Maguire, Jr., had been killed in action in Italy. Mickey, who has missed only one game all season, went out and caught her game that night.. . . . .Yesterday Mickey announced that she has received two letters from her husband, dated Aug. 1 and 8. He has suffered severe burns and was unable to write sooner, but he is very much alive. Mickey caught last night's game against Racine.

149

months later, Tom Maguire was found in Italy—alive! He had suffered severe burns while fighting.

A year after Tom came home, he and Mickey divorced, partly because he wanted her to quit baseball. Mickey played until 1949. By that time, she had married a man named George Chapman. They had six children. Their son Rick tried out for the Kansas City Royals in 1970. Mickey loved horses and trained many of them. She died on August 2, 1981.

Permissions

The author would like to acknowledge the following for use of photographs and artwork:

National Baseball Hall of Fame Library, Cooperstown, NY: 8, 65, 87; Kenosha News, 115 (first article); Larry Fritsch Cards, Inc.: 23, 32; Nina Wallace: 30, 54, 145; Northern Indiana Historical Society, Inc.: 51, 56, 70, 128; Racine Journal Times, 115 (second article).

Reproductions of baseball cards are courtesy of Larry Fritsch Cards, Inc. To get a copy of their catalog, contact them at: 735 Old Wausau Rd., P. O. Box 863, Stevens Point, WI 54481 or 715-344-8687 or www.fritschcards.com.